THE
HUNTED
HEIR

USA TODAY BESTSELLING AUTHOR

HOLLY RENEE

PRONUNCIATION GUIDE

Marmoris: MAR-moris
Enveilarian: ON-veil-air-ian
Dacre: DAY-ker
Nyra: near-ah
Wren: ren
Verena: Vuh- rehn-ah
Kai: K ai h
Eiran: AIR-in

CONTENT WARNING

For my babies, Nolan and Millie —
You are the greatest love I've ever known.

CHAPTER 1
DACRE

My father's fist slammed into my jaw with a sickening crack, instantly sending a metallic taste of blood flooding my mouth. The familiar pain spread across my face like wildfire, making it hard to focus on anything else. I closed my eyes, trying to block out the sound of his furious voice and the sting of tears in my eyes. But no matter how many times this happened, it never got easier to endure.

I could feel the heat of his rage radiating from him, his breath hot against my skin. I braced myself for another blow, but it didn't come.

My father's voice rumbled like thunder, filled with anger and disappointment. "You are a damn disgrace to this rebellion," he growled, the words dripping with disdain as he locked his gaze onto mine. "You were born to lead, yet you fell to your knees for her like a coward and let her slip through your fingers."

The weight of his disappointment felt heavy on my shoulders, crushing me with guilt as I stood there unable to defend myself.

"Pull yourself together and step out there." He gestured with a quick nod over his shoulder, and I swiftly brought my hand to my mouth to wipe away the blood that had escaped from my lip. "Don't you dare let them see any of this weakness. The rebellion looks to you for our future, Dacre."

His words were like another hit to the face, snapping me out of my daze. I straightened my posture and took a deep breath, steeling myself for what was to come.

I walked out of the warrior quarters, away from my father's piercing gaze that seemed to follow me even as I left. The tension in the air was palpable as I made my way outside, where I knew the rest of the rebellion was gathered.

They were all aware my father had an important announcement to make, but I dreaded them finding out the truth. My steps felt weighted with the heaviness of impending doom as I approached the group, their faces a mix of anticipation and apprehension.

My eyes scanned the crowd, picking out familiar faces and trying to avoid the curious stares. I finally spotted Kai and Wren standing near the front, their gazes locked on me.

Wren's narrowed eyes showed her disappointment, already aware of my betrayal, but it wasn't just her knowing look that made me uncomfortable; it was the throbbing pain in my jaw and the dried blood on my split lip that her eyes didn't veer from.

As I approached, she lifted her hand as if to touch my jaw. I flinched and swiftly swatted her hand away, before turning and keeping my gaze fixed forward. The air seemed to thicken around us like a heavy fog. My heart raced in my chest, unsure of what our father would do.

"He did this?" Wren's voice hissed through clenched teeth, trembling with emotion.

"It's not a big deal, Wren."

Kai stood beside me, his normally calm demeanor replaced with a fiery anger. His fists were clenched so tightly that his knuckles turned white as he glared up at my jaw.

He already knew what happened with Verena; he knew who she was, but even as the memory of Verena's betrayal burned in his mind, it wasn't the source of his simmering ire. Every ounce of fury was directed at the man who led the rebellion that expected blind loyalty.

But I couldn't find that allegiance with the taste of blood coating my tongue.

This wasn't the first time Kai had witnessed my father's violence toward me, and I was sure it wouldn't be the last. Even though years had passed since the first time he'd seen it, it never got any easier for him to stomach.

We had always been protective of one another, ever since we were children growing up in the rebellion together, and now, as adults fighting for our cause, that protectiveness had only grown stronger.

The faint rustle of whispers surrounded us as my father

exited the warrior quarters, Reed close on his heels. I could see the anger burning in Wren's eyes and the tension in her body as she struggled to contain it.

My father's hand rose up in a commanding gesture, silencing the commotion around us. I clenched my teeth and forced myself to stay still despite the throbbing pain in my jaw.

My father's bitter voice echoed through the cave as he stood before us, his face twisted in a familiar rage. "The heir to the Marmoris Kingdom is on the run."

A sudden cascade of murmurs and shocked gasps erupted around us. My heart raced as I couldn't focus on anything other than what he had just said, the weight of his words heavy in the air. He hadn't referred to her by name, but instead as the heir.

Because that was all she was to him.

"And she has been hiding within our ranks."

The room erupted into chaos, voices rising in confusion and astonishment, but I just continued to stare ahead at my father.

My father's eyes swept over each of us, his gaze lingering on me before moving on.

"For weeks, Nyra has been secretly training with our warriors," my father continued, his voice filled with disgust. "We're not sure if she was sent by the king or acting of her own accord."

The room fell silent at the mention of Nyra's name.

My father's gaze shifted to me, his eyes boring into mine as if he were searching for something.

"I want all of you to search for her," he commanded. "Bring her to me."

I could feel the others watching me, the weight of their eyes bearing down on me like a branding iron searing through my skin. I could feel the disappointment radiating from them, each gaze sharp and accusing.

"The future of our rebellion depends on finding her!" My father's voice reached a fevered pitch. I held my breath, having no damn clue what he would say next. The air around us crackled with tension as we stood like the soldiers he demanded us to be, waiting for his next spiteful words. "The king will do anything in his power and use every resource to find her. We should have never been so careless to let her escape."

His eyes locked onto mine, sharp and penetrating like daggers.

Guilt gnawed at me as I held his gaze. But the weight of the truth was what bore down on me until I felt like I would suffocate. My father didn't need my truth. I'd been the one to let her run. I had fucked her like she meant nothing to me and let her run.

But all he knew was that I had allowed her to get away.

My father knew she wouldn't have stood a chance at escaping unless I allowed it, and I had.

And that was the only truth he needed.

But I didn't regret it.

Regret flooded my veins like poison, but not for letting her go. I couldn't force myself to regret that.

"The princess is to be found and brought back to me. I don't care if the life has been drained from her body or if she's barely breathing. We do not allow the heir to get back to the palace."

Wren snarled, her eyes blazing with anger as she stared at our father, but he didn't spare her a glance. Verena had been the first person I had seen Wren open up to since our mother's death, and now she was gone.

And I could feel Wren's allegiance to our father wavering with every word he spoke against her. It didn't matter that Verena had lied to her as well. She was her friend.

I had expected this reaction from our power-hungry father, but I couldn't let myself think about a single one of them laying a finger on her because if they fucking hurt her... I cracked my neck in an attempt to calm myself down.

She was a fucking traitor. I knew that to be true. She was a little traitor, and she lied to me over and over again. She lied to all of us, and I was so damn angry, even if I couldn't blame her for doing so.

I was unsure if anything she had told me was true, if anything I had felt...

Fuck.

I couldn't let myself go there. Not now.

Not when my father was already looking at me as if I had betrayed him in a way that no one else ever had.

But even as I tried to push her lies and her soft moans from my mind, I couldn't push her out completely. I couldn't stop thinking about the way she had looked at me when her true name slipped past my lips. The look of betrayal in her eyes as she stared back at me before running from my room.

The scars on her back were the last damn thing I saw as she ran from me.

Her father. That was what she told me. Her father was the one who had given her those scars, and I believed her, even now, even if it had only been a half-truth.

She told me it was her father, but she failed to mention it was the king.

The mere thought of the king sent a surge of primal rage coursing through my veins. Images of retribution and blood-red vengeance consumed my mind, overshadowing any previous hatred I had for the man.

I wanted him to beg for my mercy and struggle for breaths under my grip as I tightened my hand around his throat. I wanted to feel his fear beneath my fingers as I watched the life slowly drain from his eyes.

I had never wanted someone's blood on my hands in the way that I craved his.

Because I had never wanted to protect someone as badly as I wanted to protect her. And that thought left me torn and unsettled. She was the last person who deserved my protection.

A sharp pain stabbed my chest as the thought crept into my mind, but I gritted my teeth and pushed it away.

"We will divide our efforts and scour every corner of the kingdom. We won't leave a single stone unturned until she is found. If anyone is found harboring her, kill them. Just bring her to me!"

Many nodded their heads at my father's instructions, but I didn't. I would find her, but it wouldn't be for the benefit of him, or this rebellion.

Reed spoke close to my father's ear, drawing his attention away from the crowd who began murmuring among themselves.

The pounding of my heart echoed in my ears as I dug my nails into my palms. With every thought of her, the loyalty that had become so ingrained in who I was slipped further from my grip. I was the rebellion leader's son, but she had wrecked everything I knew.

My mind was in utter chaos. Anger, betrayal, regret. My mother had sacrificed everything for this cause, for this rebellion. My whole life had been molded for what was to come once we won, yet the only thought that continued to run through my head was, W*hy didn't I go with her?*

A whirl of tangled, conflicting thoughts fought and clawed at each other, causing my head to throb.

But one thing was clear, I would not let my father find her.

My gaze was pulled toward my sister, her arms crossed tightly over her chest as she looked up at me. The intensity of her glare made me shift uncomfortably, like I was suddenly standing on a wire that could break at any moment.

"I'm going to find her." My voice came out in a strained, determined tone, more forceful than I had intended to allow myself.

The corners of her eyes crinkled in fury, and I could

feel the heat of her anger radiating toward me as if I could reach out and touch it.

"I don't want you to find her." She moved closer to me, and I felt Kai shift at my side. "I don't want you or our father anywhere near her."

"Don't lump me with him."

"Why not?" She raised an eyebrow and leaned back, her sharp eyes scanning me up and down. "It seems like you've been taking your training with him seriously. You're truly beginning to resemble the man," she said, her tone dripping with venom.

And she hit her mark.

We both knew I had no real idea about who I wanted to be in this world, but I was absolutely certain that I didn't want to be anything like him.

I could see my father turn to look at us out of the corner of my eye, but I tried to ignore him. "I am nothing like him."

"Then you find her." Wren narrowed the distance between us and jabbed her index finger into my chest. "You find her and don't you dare bring her back here, Dacre."

I stared down at my sister, and I was about to open my mouth, when our father interrupted us.

"Dacre, you are with me." His words were laced with a tone of authority, one that I had grown accustomed to over the years.

"Kai, Wren, and I were just discussing our plan to head out on the search," I lied, but I knew neither of them would disagree with me.

Wren could be mad at me all she wanted, but she'd always have my back.

"That's not going to happen. You are with me. Kai and Wren will be staying in the city until we return."

Wren squared her shoulders, preparing for another round of arguing, but when her gaze met mine, I gently shook my head.

This wasn't a battle we wanted, not when there would still be a war to fight.

"What's the plan?" I asked, trying to sound as if I wasn't ready to burn this entire damn kingdom to the ground before I'd let him touch her.

My father's eyes narrowed. "We'll head north first. The princess will most likely be trying to get back into the palace. We need to be prepared to stop her."

"She's not going to the palace." I spoke without thinking, but even if I was with my father, I couldn't waste time heading north when I knew Verena would be heading as far away from the palace as she could get.

"Did she tell you that when you let her run?" my father snapped, his nostrils flaring.

I clenched my fists, trying to hide my frustration.

"No, but I know her better than that," I replied, meeting his gaze head-on. "She's not stupid. She knows the palace is where we'd be looking for her."

Another lie for the little traitor.

I shouldn't have been lying *for* her. I shouldn't have cared about where she was at all, but I fucking did.

My father's expression hardened. "She won't last long

out there. We'll find her. We won't stop until she's captured and brought back here."

"We will." I agreed with my father for the first time in a long time. I was going to find her, but I wouldn't be bringing her back here.

CHAPTER 2
VERENA

My legs screamed in protest as I ascended another steep hill, sweat dripping down my forehead and stinging my eyes. But it was nothing compared to the gnawing pain in my stomach that twisted and turned until I felt like I couldn't breathe.

I knew I couldn't keep going like this and needed to find shelter and food soon before exhaustion and hunger overtook me completely. For three days, I had pushed through without rest or sustenance, and my body was now fiercely protesting.

Still, I pressed on, taking slow, deliberate steps as I scanned the horizon for any signs of civilization. My eyes were drawn to the distance, where a haze of smoke hung in the air. It could only mean one thing: a village.

I quickened my pace, my heart pounding with hope and anticipation as I descended the incline, the smoke growing thicker and more visible.

It would be a risk to stop, but it would be an even bigger risk if I didn't find something to eat soon.

I had attempted to use my bow and arrows to hunt a rabbit earlier, but I couldn't tell if it was my own hesitation over taking a life or my lack of proficiency that caused me to fail miserably.

Or if it was the way my mind drifted to Dacre and the way he had touched me when he taught me to use it.

Either way, I was left with no rabbit and a growing hunger.

I was still wearing the same leathers I left the hidden city in, the ones I left Dacre in. They would know I wasn't just some girl who was traveling through. I looked like I belonged to the rebellion that I was certain was now looking for me.

He would be looking for me.

My father was an enemy of the rebellion, and now, so was I.

The village was nestled in a small valley, a cluster of scattered houses and buildings surrounded by a dense forest. Smoke curled from the chimneys of the homes, and I heard the low murmur of voices.

As I approached the entrance of the village, I paused, my heart beating wildly in my chest.

I kept my head down as I walked, trying to blend in with the villagers mingling about, going about their daily tasks. An older lady knelt over a bed of blooming vegetables, her hands caked in the same dirt that splattered across her tattered apron. She glanced up at me as I passed, and our eyes met briefly, before I quickly looked away.

I didn't want any trouble in this village; I just needed food and a few minutes to rest so I could figure out my next move.

My steps echoed through the narrow, winding streets, each one a reminder of the growing ache in my stomach. I followed the plume of smoke rising from a nearby cottage, my feet taking me closer and closer to its source. As I neared the quaint tavern, I noticed its wooden door propped open, as if beckoning me inside with the promise of food and rest.

I stepped inside, my senses immediately assaulted by the warm, musty smell of ale and sweat. A low murmur of conversation filled the room as I looked around, my eyes darting around the sparsely littered tables in the dimly lit cottage.

A burly man stood behind the bar, his unruly beard reaching his chest as he wiped down the wooden bartop in front of him. He gave me a curious once-over before turning back to his customer, who sat on an old stool and leaned forward on his elbows as if the bar was responsible for holding him upright.

Taking a deep breath to steady my nerves, I awkwardly made my way over to the bar, trying to hide my trembling hands and shaky resolve.

My heart raced as I pulled out a stool and took a seat.

I reached into my pocket and felt the weight of the single coin I had left. Today was the day I would spend it.

"What can I get you?" The barkeep moved until he stood behind the bar in front of me, his rough hands resting on its surface. He cleared his throat, drawing my attention. My eyes shot up to meet his, the deep smile lines creasing around his eyes in stark contrast to the scruff on his face.

"What can I get you?" he asked gruffly, repeating himself, but he softened his tone.

I swallowed nervously, trying to gather my thoughts. I needed food.

"Do you have any food?" I asked tentatively, my voice barely above a whisper.

The barkeep's eyebrows drew together slightly, and I couldn't miss the way his gaze roamed over me as if he was assessing exactly who I was with that one look.

"Not much, but we have stew and some day-old bread."

Relief washed over me as I pulled out the coin and placed it on the counter. "Is this enough?"

He caught my wrist in his firm grip, causing me to jump in surprise. I felt his fingers press against the counterfeit rebellion mark that I had foolishly gotten tattooed on my skin.

The mark that had led me to *him*.

My heart pounded against my rib cage as he looked over my mark. I could only imagine what thoughts raced through his mind as he held my pulsing wrist in his hand.

Did he know I was on the run? Did he know my true identity? I feared with the rebellion on the hunt for me that word may have already spread through the villages.

With a gentle yet commanding gesture, he extended his other hand toward me. As he turned his wrist, the faded lines of his own rebellion mark came into view. The intri-

cate design and meaning behind it were now exposed for
me to see.

As I stared at the mark etched into his skin, I should
have calmed with a sense of familiarity and security, but
instead, a heavy wave of dread washed over me.

Dacre had taken what had started to feel like home and
twisted it into something cruel and unforgiving. The hidden
city had become something that would see me dead just as
my father would.

My chest ached as I stared down at this man's mark and
all I could see was Dacre's betrayal. All I could see was my
own.

He had called me a little traitor since the day I met
him, and he was right. I had been betraying him all
along.

But I couldn't have trusted him with the truth.

He was the son of the rebellion, and I was the daughter
of everything they fought against. We were born and bred
to be enemies, to never trust the other.

The barkeep cocked his head to the side, studying me
intently. I felt uncomfortable under his watchful gaze. It
was as if he could see right through me, unraveling all my
secrets and fears. His scrutiny made me squirm, and I
longed to escape.

But I longed for food more.

"Who are you running from?" he asked, breaking the
tense silence between us.

I felt my heart drop into my stomach as panic flooded
through my body.

Without thinking, I stood and started to back away from

him, my hand instinctively reaching for the knife that was tucked into my vest.

I had no power, hadn't been able to feel a single stirring of it since I left the hidden city. It was only my dagger and I that could protect me now.

But instead of attacking me or calling attention to me like I expected, the barkeep's expression softened and he held up his hands in a calming gesture.

"Easy now, no need for that."

My mind raced as I tried to come up with an explanation or excuse so I could get out of here.

"Sit down and eat." He nodded back to the stool I had just left. "You're not going to make it much farther if you don't get some food in you."

When I didn't move, he sighed and leaned forward on the bar so he was looking directly at me and no one else could hear him.

"You'll find that most people here have no support for the king, but our support for the rebellion is wavering as well."

My gaze snapped up to meet his, and I let out a shaky breath. "What?"

He motioned for me once again to take a seat, and this time I did as he said.

I sat down on the stool, my hand still resting on the knife. The barkeep walked to the back, and my spine straightened as I watched the direction he just left before scanning the small tavern to see if anyone else was looking at me.

The barkeep returned, his hands full with a steaming

bowl of stew and a chunk of bread. He set them both down before me and nodded.

I didn't wait.

I grabbed the spoon and shoved a large bite of stew into my mouth. I didn't care that it burned my tongue. I was starving.

"Slow down or you'll make yourself sick."

He took a small step back before pouring me an ale and sliding it onto the bar in front of me.

I quickly swallowed my food and reached for the glass.

"How did you know?"

"That you're on the run?" He chuckled, the sound deep and carefree.

I nodded, and he crossed his arms.

"Well, I know you aren't just passing through. Nobody just passes through here, especially not when they look like they are on the verge of passing out from hunger."

He leaned in closer, his eyes piercing into mine.

"Besides," he continued, "I saw the mark on your wrist when you first walked in. It's not one that many people show off so carelessly, especially not when the king's soldiers just tore through our town looking for the lost heir."

I swallowed hard, my throat dry with fear.

"I need to leave."

"You need to eat." He nodded toward my stew. "The king's soldiers left two nights ago, and they were headed south, which I assume is the same direction you're heading."

I nodded even though I had no reason to trust him.

"Then you'll eat and rest." He said it so matter-of-factly, as if there was no room for argument, and there wasn't. I couldn't tell this man that I was not only running from the king's soldiers but also the men who were meant to protect those who didn't serve the king.

I took another bite of food before thinking about what he had said. "What did you mean by the support for the rebellion is wavering?"

He studied me for a long moment before answering.

"The rebellion was never supposed to be about power or control. It was a fight for freedom, for a better future. But as time has passed, some have started to see it as an opportunity for power. The lines have become blurred, and many have lost sight of the true meaning."

I absorbed his words, letting my thoughts drift to Dacre's father. I had felt uneasy since the first moment I met him, and I now knew it was because he reminded me of someone else.

My father.

Power-hungry men who lost sight of what should have been important to them.

I looked down at my stew and bread before taking another bite and savoring the warmth it brought to my empty stomach.

Dacre could be one of those men too, but a flicker of doubt told me that even though I wanted to hate him, he was nothing like them.

And that somehow made things so much worse than if he was.

Both my betrayal and his would have been easier to

stomach if he had fit into the mold I had created in my mind. But instead, he turned out to be nothing like I imagined. The realization hit me like a wave crashing against the shore, leaving me lost and confused in its wake.

I looked up at the barkeep, his eyes still on me, waiting for me to respond.

"I've met men like that," I managed to choke out, my voice barely above a whisper.

He sighed, running a hand through his beard as he spoke. "I'd say you have. It's hard to trust anyone anymore, and even those who led the fight for a better future have become blinded by their ambitions."

I looked down at my half-finished meal, feeling the weight of his words bearing down on me.

"You think Davian wants to become king."

He clenched his jaw as if he shouldn't have said what he said next, and I wish he hadn't.

"It has been Davian's plan for years to make his son, Dacre, the next heir to the throne."

My stomach twisted with a mix of anger and something I couldn't place. I thought they were fighting for a better life, fighting against my ruthless father, but in reality, they were doing nothing more than helping Dacre secure his place as the next king.

Beyond my father, I was the only other person standing in his way.

And yet, he had let me run.

If his father found me, I had no doubt that he would see me dead.

I took another bite of my food, swallowing it down and dropping the spoon back into the bowl.

"Thank you for this." I nodded down to the food as I stood. "I need to leave."

He watched me carefully, too carefully, but he didn't try to stop me.

Instead, he simply nodded once as I stood and walked out the door.

CHAPTER 3
DACRE

Darkness blanketed the forest as we pushed forward. It had been two days since I followed my father out of the city, and in those two days, we had seen little signs of Verena.

Occasionally, we'd catch a glimpse of what looked like faint footprints in the soft soil, but they'd disappear as if the forest itself was trying to conceal her.

But we had seen the king's soldiers.

We had trailed after them, as silent as ghosts through the dense woods. Eiran's sharp ears caught snippets of conversation—whispers about her, about how she had been seen in a nearby village.

The king was after her. They were hunting her down just as we were, and I feared what he would do if he got his hands on her.

When I found her, she had been in the dungeons. His own daughter locked up like a beast.

I had assumed then that she was like any other traitor fleeing the kingdom with a fake rebellion mark on her arm, and I had treated her as such. But I couldn't ignore the possibility of something much darker lurking behind her escape.

I was haunted by memories of her scars, and each one ignited a fire of anger within me.

Each scar was a secret she kept hidden from the world, etched into her skin like a map of her past. They curled and twisted into one another, each one hiding her pain as if they could disguise it.

And I felt possessed with the urge to trace each one and find out her truths.

"We need to stop for the night," my father grunted. With every hour that passed without finding her, he grew more volatile as did my unease.

There were five of us in total. My father, Eiran, and my father's two right-hand men, Adler, and Eiran's father, Reed.

And every one of them followed my father with a blind allegiance.

If he wanted Verena, then they would do everything within their power to get her, and I would do everything within my power to stop them.

We stopped near the edge of a river, and I rolled my neck as my father squatted down and cupped the cool water in his hands. He took a long drink before he turned to me, his gaze critical even in the darkness of the night.

"We're still a few days of travel away from the southern coast."

I nodded, my mind racing with a thousand thoughts of finding her.

"If the king's men get to her before we do, they will take her back to the palace." He ran his wet hands over his face before running them along the back of his neck. "We have to get to her before they do."

I gritted my teeth as I watched him. Of course, they would take her back to the palace, but it was what her father would do with her once they got her there that worried me. She wasn't a lost princess. She was on the run.

I knew in my gut that was the truth, and I hated that I hadn't known that truth from the beginning.

I had no idea what I would have done if I had, but fuck, I had been so damn cruel to her out of my own anger. She had lied and betrayed me, but I didn't know what secrets she kept buried.

She was a traitor, but who was it that she was truly betraying?

"We won't let them get to her," Eiran promised my father as he rummaged through his pack, determination etched into every line of his face. My hands clenched into fists at my sides, the urge to lash out welling up inside me.

"What's the plan for once we get her?" I looked away from Eiran and watched my father's eyes as I asked the question.

He paused for a moment, his gaze distant as he thought about his response. "First, we find her, then we'll do exactly what needs to be done."

"Which is?" I could hear my heartbeat whooshing in

my ears. Whatever plan my father had for her, I wasn't
going to like it.

"Which is what you should have already done instead
of thinking with your cock." He let out a frustrated growl,
and I saw Eiran's irritating smirk from the corner of my
eye. "Do you honestly think I would trust you with our plan
after what you've done?"

"And do you honestly think that I'm going to help you
find her when you plan on using her like she's some sort of
bait to draw her father out?" I shouldn't have said it. I knew
I shouldn't have, and the way his eyes narrowed and his
jaw clenched only reassured me of that.

"I think you've become a liability when you're
supposed to be our future. Our people are counting on you,
and you're willing to sacrifice their future for the king's
daughter?" His words hit me like a punch to the gut. In all
my life, he had never questioned my loyalty or my ability
to be exactly what he needed me to be.

"Because I don't want you to use a girl who's done
nothing wrong?" She hadn't. Not to him anyway.

"Because you've forgotten where your loyalty should
lie!" He moved so close to me that his chest pressed against
mine.

My loyalty should have been with my family, with my
father, with the rebellion, but he was right.

My loyalty had been wavering for a long time. It
seemed to solidify the day my mother was killed, but my
father had been so consumed by his thirst for revenge and
his own agenda that he had become blinded to everything
the rebellion once stood for.

Verena had become a weapon that effortlessly shredded the last remnants of my loyalty.

And that only made me angrier at her.

I was angry at my father for the way he wanted to use her as a pawn, but had I been nothing but one to her?

Was this what she wanted all along?

Even if I had wanted to believe that to be true, the look in her eyes when I called out her true name told me it wasn't.

She had decided to stay in a rebellion that hated her father, hated everything he stood for, and she chose to train at my side and take all the bullshit I'd thrown at her as if she were willing to fight for the same things that we were.

And I had believed her.

Part of me still did.

Part of me wished that she had been exactly who she said she was instead of the one person I shouldn't have wanted, shouldn't have craved.

And that made us both fools.

"I haven't forgotten." I bit back the words that threatened to spill from my lips, words that would break the fragile trust between us. "I have spent my entire life not forgetting, just as Wren has."

He paused, his eyes searching mine as if trying to look for the lies behind my words. Finally, he let out a deep sigh before looking away.

"You're right." The tension in his voice made it clear that he didn't mean it. "We'll get the princess, and you'll do exactly what needs to be done."

He grabbed the back of my neck and pulled me forward

until my forehead touched his. "We're all counting on you, Dacre. The rebellion, our people. Don't let your mother's death be for nothing."

For nothing. As if her death in itself hadn't meant everything. Her life nor her death should have been measured in how it helped the damned rebellion, but that was what she had been reduced down to.

They idolized her, dropped to their knees and prayed to the gods to have her protect our rebellion, but none of them prayed for her soul. They prayed for her protection, while Wren and I beseeched the gods for her peace.

"We won't fail you, sir." Eiran stood and handed my father some food from his pack. "We won't fail the rebellion."

CHAPTER 4
VERENA

Less than half a day had passed since I left the tavern, but my stomach grumbled with renewed hunger.

My body had forgotten what it had been like to live on the streets and had become spoiled while living in the hidden city.

And I was paying for that now.

The sun was slowly sinking behind the dense canopy of trees, casting long shadows and splashing the sky with vibrant hues of orange and pink. As the light diminished, a dusky purple haze began to settle over the land, giving way to a blanket of darkness that enveloped everything in its path. It was as if nature itself was preparing for a slumber under the watchful eye of a starry night.

The air was still and quiet until a rustling in the bushes caught my attention. I froze, the hairs on the back of my neck standing on end. Slowly, I reached for my dagger, my fingers wrapping around the handle.

My heart pounded as I squatted and scanned the under-growth, searching for any sign of movement. But there was nothing, just the sound of my heavy, labored breathing and the soft crunch of leaves underfoot as I slowly backed away.

Pulling myself back to my feet, I took off, heading south as quickly as I could. The instinct to keep moving, to stay ahead of danger, was a familiar one, but my exhaustion plagued my limbs with every step I took.

The scent of damp earth and pine permeated the air, and I could feel the chill seeping into my bones as night fell.

My heavy-lidded eyes blinked closed, my weary body stumbling through the dense forest. Exhaustion was drag-ging me down, but I knew I had to keep going, putting as much distance between myself and whoever was coming for me.

Because they were coming for me.

They all would be.

The trees loomed overhead, their gnarled branches reaching out like hands in the dim light of the moon.

My feet trudged along the damp ground, squelching with each step as though the earth was trying to pull me under. I needed rest, my senses and movements were becoming lazy and far too loud, but I couldn't risk stopping.

Every rustle of leaves and snap of twigs set my heart racing, wondering if it was just an animal or something more sinister. But I couldn't stop, not until I reached safety, wherever that may be.

I pressed my hand against the trunk of the nearest tree,

pausing for only a moment to catch my breath. The shadows grew thicker and the air colder as I continued at a much slower pace.

My body was tired, but it was my mind that plagued me. I couldn't think straight when I lacked sleep, and thoughts of my mother crept up into my head when I normally was so equipped with forcing them down.

Her face swam before my eyes, the same soft smile that she always had. She had been my best friend once upon a time, my only friend, and now, she was gone.

She was gone because my father wanted another heir, needed an heir with power. He had demanded it of her, and now she was gone.

Thoughts of Dacre flooded my mind, of his own mother. Was she so different from my own? They both died for their families, for their people. They both died trying to protect what they loved.

My mother trying to provide a future heir for our kingdom.

His trying to replace me with an heir of their own.

They had both given everything for the greed of the one they loved.

I had been able to see it in Dacre's father's eyes from the moment I met him. It was the same look my father always held, but I had been foolish when it came to Dacre.

I hadn't seen it with him.

I hadn't felt it.

My mother would be ashamed of me. Ashamed that I ran from our home, from my duty.

And I ran straight into the hands of our enemy, into the

hands of the one who would destroy everything I once loved.

My mind raced with thoughts and memories, making it difficult to focus on my surroundings, but the sound of twigs snapping jolted me back to reality.

I tightened my hand around my dagger as I scanned the darkness around me.

It was all-encompassing, a thick veil that enveloped everything in its path. Shapes and shadows danced in the blackness, but nothing was distinguishable between the trees.

It was toying with me and feeding my fear as if it were as starved as I felt.

I gasped for air, my chest heaving as I frantically took in my surroundings. But before I could fully process my panic, a large hand clamped over my mouth, muffling my cries. I stumbled backward and collided with a hard, unyielding body pressed against me from behind.

"Shhh," a voice whispered in my ear, the sound far too close for comfort.

Dacre. His name raced through my mind as my heart pounded against my ribs. I squirmed, trying to land my dagger into the person behind me, but they caught my wrist before I could even attempt to do any damage.

His hand clamped down tighter around my mouth, and a muffled "Shit" slipped from his lips just as I heard voices coming from the direction I had just come.

I took a deep, ragged breath through my nose, as my hands trembled.

"Where the hell did she go?"

The shadows seemed to amplify the beating of my heart, the sound deafening as my chest rose and fell rapidly. My hands shook as I gripped my dagger tightly, trying to regain control.

"Her tracks led this way, but the forest is too dense now." Another man spoke and fear snaked a slow path down my spine, coiling around every part of me until I couldn't escape it.

"We need to head farther south." A third. "Gods know that's where she's headed, and the king will have all of our heads if she manages to board a ship before we can get our hands on her."

My father's men.

I tried to breathe through my nose, but the task became harder and harder as they finally came into view through the dappled moonlight, and I spotted the uniforms I had been surrounded by my whole life.

"Quiet." The voice behind me was so hushed that I barely heard him, but still, I listened.

I nodded, swallowing the lump of fear in my throat.

I was silent as we listened to the king's soldiers push forward through the forest. My eyes darted around the darkness, the trees looming above us like dark, foreboding sentinels.

This forest held my secrets, and I was terrified that it would give me away.

For a few moments, we stood still and frozen, listening to the retreating sounds of the soldiers until they were swallowed up by the rustling leaves. Slowly, his fingers loosened their tight grasp on me and I stumbled away, my feet tripping over roots and rocks in my haste to put distance between us. When I finally turned to face him, my body was shaking with adrenaline and my heart was pounding so hard against my chest I was sure he could hear it. My breath came in short gasps as I struggled to steady myself.

"Eiran." My voice was like a butterfly's wings, delicate and elusive, fluttering softly in the dark.

The wave of disappointment that crashed over me was cold and heavy. It wasn't Dacre. He hadn't come.

Eiran's eyes were hard and unyielding, but there was a flicker of something else beneath the surface. He stepped forward, the moonlight casting eerie shadows across his face.

"We need to talk," he said, his voice low and almost unrecognizable.

It reminded me of Micah, of the way the two of us would huddle close together and speak in hushed tones, afraid someone would overhear us. It had been so long since I last thought of him.

Guilt washed over me, drowning me in shame.

He had been my only friend after I left the palace, and I had barely allowed myself to think of him since I was taken by the palace guards.

I had trusted him when I couldn't trust anyone else, and I selfishly wished he were here with me now. I pressed my thumb against the mark he had given me, the fake mark that he believed would help me escape.

I shook my head, hardly trusting my voice to speak the words that swirled inside me. "I don't trust you."

As if walking on quicksand, my feet sunk deeper and

deeper into the ground with each step I took away from
him, the mistrust bubbling up within me and forcing me to
retreat.

Why was he here?

He lifted his hands as if he were surrendering in front of
me, his eyes never leaving mine. "I came here to find you.
Not to serve Davian."

I shot him a look of utter disbelief, my brow furrowing.
With my back pressed against the rough bark of the tree
behind me, I could feel the texture of the wood digging into
my palms as I braced myself. "Your father serves Davian."

"And yours has destroyed our kingdom." He cocked his
head to the side, his eyes not wavering from mine. "Are we
to be judged by the sins of our fathers? I promise you,
Princess, you will lose."

"Don't call me that," I snapped, my voice echoing off
the trees, too loud and too sharp.

Eiran's eyebrow shot up in a silent display of surprise.
His words had struck a nerve deep within me, but I knew
he was speaking the truth. The weight of my father's sins
hung heavily on my shoulders.

If I were to be judged for my father's sins, there was no
chance our people would allow me to live.

My voice quivered as I spoke, the fear and uncertainty
evident in my tone. "You could be lying," I accused him,
my eyes searching his face for any sign of deception.

He responded with a cold, hard stare. "You have been,"
he countered, his words hitting me like a punch to the gut.
My chest ached as he continued, "And now the entire rebellion is after you."

Desperately, I pressed my hands into the rough bark of the tree behind me, digging my fingers in until my knuckles turned white with the force. "Except for you?"

He drew nearer, his face coming into focus under the soft glow of the moon. Every line and curve were visible to me, from the slight creases around his eyes to the sharp line of his jaw. The moonlight danced through the branches above, casting shadows across his features as he leaned in closer.

Eiran hesitated, his eyes searching for the answer in my own. "Yes." His lips barely moved as he spoke, the muscles of his jaw taut. "Except for me."

I watched him intently, scouring his face for any hint of deception in his words. But the weariness that consumed me threatened to cloud my judgment and I struggled to maintain my focus. My eyelids felt heavy as lead, weighing down my every movement.

"I haven't trusted Dacre for years, and I didn't trust him with you."

"You don't even know me."

He shook his head, his jaw clenching as he struggled to contain his emotions. "You've never given me a chance to."

I hadn't given that chance to anyone.

My thoughts went to Wren, and I winced at the thought of all the lies I had fed her, the deceit that had become second nature to me.

I had lied to them all.

I blinked; my thoughts scrambled. My gaze wandered down to my feet, unsure of what to say. Finally, I lifted my head to meet his intense stare, feeling a surge of emotions rising within me. "Why are you doing this?"

Eiran took a deep breath, his eyes never leaving mine. "Because they are going to kill you if you don't get away."

His words struck me like a bolt of lightning. I had known deep down that this would happen, but hearing it spoken aloud by someone made it all too real. The air around us seemed to crackle with tension, an invisible storm brewing between us.

"Kill me?"

With the moonlight dancing upon his face, his eyes reflected all the weight and solemnity of his words. There was no room for doubt or deception in his gaze, only an unshakable conviction that sent shivers down my spine. "If the rebellion finds you, Davian will see you dead. If your father's men find you, I fear what he will do."

"My father." Cold fear twisted in my heart.

"He's announced an award for your return, Nyra." Eiran's eyes were fixed on my face, studying every movement and flicker of emotion that passed through me. "The entire kingdom knows you're missing. They know of the queen's death."

My heart raced and my palms were slick with sweat. Every muscle in my body tensed, ready to flee at a moment's notice. The looming threat of the rebellion seemed insignificant compared to the danger that my own father could bring upon me.

"What did you say?" My voice trembled as I spoke, betraying the terror that consumed me.

"There's a reward."

"No." I shook my head. "The queen?"

Eiran's expression turned grim. "Yes." He nodded. "The details of her death are unclear, but it was rumored that she was expecting another heir."

My heart sank at the confirmation of my worst fears. The queen was dead, her heir.

A sense of eerie familiarity washed over me as the memories of my mother flooded back. The weight of her pain and suffering hit me in the chest like a physical blow.

She had been pushed to her breaking point by the constant pressure to produce another heir for the king, and now, history was repeating itself with the new queen, who had also fallen victim to his ruthless demands.

"I need to go." I pushed off the tree, but my feet were unsteady. Eiran reached out and wrapped his hands around my arms, and he leaned down until we were looking at one another eye to eye.

"You need to rest." His gaze searched my body, and I hated to think about what he was seeing. "You might as well just give yourself over to them if you think you're going to be able to continue like this."

"I will be fine."

"You have no power, Nyra."

I swallowed hard. *Dacre hadn't told them.*

And Dacre wasn't here. Eiran was.

How had he found me? How did he get away from the rebellion in order to do so?

"You look like you're going to pass out at any second. We need to find some shelter and let you get some rest. You should know better."

My spine straightened, and I balled my hand into a fist. "I didn't exactly have that option, Eiran."

"Well, I'm here now." Eiran's expression softened, lines of worry and exhaustion etched on his face as he looked at me. "You have options now."

CHAPTER 5
DACRE

I stirred awake to the low, hushed hum of murmuring voices and groaned. The sky was still shrouded in the darkness of predawn, but the others were already stirring, eager to begin the search once more.

And I was just as eager.

Despite my reluctance, I had finally allowed myself to succumb to the exhaustion that had been clawing at my body. My father insisted on taking over watch so I could rest, and I had drifted off into a fitful sleep.

The cool morning dew stuck to my cheeks, and I reached up my hand instinctively, wiping the droplets away as I sat up. We were camped just outside the village that Verena had supposedly been spotted in, and anticipation coursed through me at the thought of finally finding a sign of her.

She was out there somewhere, alone and vulnerable, and guilt twisted inside of me for failing to protect her. The mere thought of what she could be enduring made my gut churn with worry.

It was my fault.

My father's gaze turned toward me, his expression stern and worried as he observed me through tired eyes.

I forced myself to stand despite the protests from my exhausted body.

"What's happened?" I asked, my voice still hoarse with sleep.

"The queen is dead." The words hung heavily in the air, shrouding me in a blanket of unease.

"What?" I ran my fingers through my hair, feeling the tangles from sleeping on the forest floor. "How do you know?"

Questions churned in my mind, each one more pressing than the last.

"Eiran snuck into the village last night after I began watch. He overheard the villagers talking."

Eiran. I turned away from my father, looking for him, but he was no longer in the camp.

"Where is he?"

A surge of dread washed over me. The death of the queen could only mean one thing—the king wouldn't stop until he found Verena.

With the queen dead, she was his only heir.

"The king?" he replied. "In mourning, I would assume. Though I doubt the man mourns very long. He lost the queen, but it's rumored he lost an unborn child as well."

My stomach churned as I processed the implications of the queen's death. The news brought a new wave of urgency to the search for Verena. I needed to find Verena before anyone else could.

"Where is Eiran?" I grabbed the small pack of supplies I had brought with me, adjusting the straps over my shoulder.

My father shifted uncomfortably, avoiding my gaze as he answered my question. His eyes flicked to the south. "I sent him back to the hidden city. He's gone to warn the others of what's coming."

Suspicion and doubt clouded my thoughts when it came to Eiran. It had been years since I last trusted him, and now a sickening unease crept into my gut.

"Why didn't you wake me?" I couldn't control the bite of anger in my voice.

"The village wasn't going to wake before the sunrise so there was no need to wake you," he replied calmly. "Despite the news of a dead queen, we still need to find out what they know of the princess, about where she went."

I nodded, the weight of the situation bearing down on me. The urgency to find Verena intensified, knowing that the king would stop at nothing to track her down. I didn't know the king's motivations, couldn't fathom what the man was planning, but Verena was the heir to this kingdom, the heir to his power.

And with the news of the queen's death spreading like wildfire, the stakes had been raised even higher.

Without another word, I set off toward the village, my father's voice fading into the background as my determination propelled me forward.

The early morning mist clung to the trees, creating an eerie atmosphere that matched the turmoil in my chest.

When I reached the outskirts of the village, I slowed my pace, scanning the surroundings.

The villagers were just beginning to stir, unaware of the storm brewing in their midst.

They moved about their daily routines, but there was an undercurrent of fear that set my teeth on edge. I strained to catch pieces of hushed conversations that might offer a clue to Verena's whereabouts.

My eyes landed on an elderly woman whispering frantically to a younger man.

I edged closer, careful not to draw too much attention to myself. Their voices were low, but I managed to catch fragments of their conversation.

"…queen's death…" the woman murmured, her voice tinged with sorrow.

"…princess…" Another trail of whispers.

I inched closer, and the woman shot me a cautious look before leaning in to whisper something into the man's ear. His eyes widened as he turned fully to face me.

"Have you seen a young woman?" I asked foolishly, and she grunted.

"Are you here looking for the princess?" She crossed her arms, her wrinkled skin creasing around her eyes.

The man beside her tensed, looking ready to bolt.

"I am." I quickly looked over my shoulder, but I saw no signs of my father.

"Your men have already raided our village looking for her. She's not here." Deep frown lines creased her forehead, conveying her defiance. "Tell your king he'll have to look somewhere else."

"I serve no king."

The woman narrowed her eyes farther. "So you're after her for the reward."

It wasn't a question.

"What reward?" I asked, trying to keep my voice steady despite the urgency pulsing through my veins.

"The king has offered a reward for the princess's safe return. He reports she was captured from the palace."

Taken. Not escaped. The king would never risk tarnishing his power by letting the public know that the princess had fled from him. He was too cunning, too sly to let anyone believe that he had lost control over his subjects or his own family.

His own heir.

"Captured?"

"By the rebellion." She watched me carefully, his eyes roaming over my leathers and the weapons strapped to my body. "They say the rebellion is to blame for the queen's death as well."

"How?" I demanded.

The young man leaned in now, his voice so quiet I could barely hear him. "It's said the rebellion sent an assassin into the palace disguised as a servant. The queen was found dead in her chamber and the princess nowhere to be seen."

More lies. More deceit.

I could hear commotion coming from behind me, and I watched a villager slam their door as my father and his men appeared from the line of trees.

"You're with them." It was an accusation.

"Have you seen the princess?" I rushed, wanting more information, needing more.

I reached forward, wrapping my hand around hers. As our hands touched, I could feel the warmth radiating from the woman's palm, a comforting heat that spread through my own. Her skin was soft and slightly calloused, and I could feel the gentle pressure of her grip against my own. "Please help me find her before they do. She's in danger."

Her eyes locked onto mine, their sharp, calculating gaze like an arrow piercing straight through me. They were a deep, rich brown, and every crease and contour of her irises was etched with stories and secrets. "There was a young woman who passed through two days ago. I don't know much, but she stopped at the tavern."

My father's hand came down on my shoulder, startling me, and I quickly turned to face him, his expression inscrutable as he studied the elderly woman before us.

"What did you learn?"

The woman's gaze flickered between my father and me, her lips pressed into a thin line. "I've told him everything we know." She put her hand out in front of her companion as if she needed to suddenly shield him.

"A young woman passed through here a few days ago," I quickly answered. Telling as much truth as I could.

My every step felt like walking on a tightrope, teetering between revealing just enough truth to stay on track in our search for her and fabricating enough lies to ensure that I would be the one to find her first.

"We need to question more of the village to see what we can find." My father's keen eyes remained fixed on the woman, and she didn't cower under his stare.

"I agree." I nodded. "We have a lot of ground to cover."

The four of us split up, each of heading in a different direction. I quickly made my way toward the town's tavern, eager to uncover any clues that might lead us to where she went.

As I stepped inside, the air was thick with the smell of stale ale and smoke. There was only one other patron inside, a disheveled man who looked like he may have spent the entire night inside.

Another man stood behind the bar, tirelessly wiping down the surface. His round eyes widened as he saw me enter, and I quickly made my way over to him.

"Excuse me, sir," I began, trying to sound as non-threatening as possible. "I'm looking for a woman who may have passed through here a couple days ago. One of the village women told me she saw her come in here."

"Dacre?" His hand abruptly stopped, frozen in midair, as he stared at me with a look of utter disbelief etched on his face.

"I'm sorry. Do I know you?" I studied the man's face, trying to recall if I had ever seen him before. His skin was weathered, and a slight scar ran down his cheek. Despite my efforts, I couldn't place him in my memory.

"It's been many years since I've seen you." He dropped the rag before running his hands down his shirt. "Why are you here?"

"I'm looking for Princess Verena."

His eyes darted around the tavern even though there was no one else there, but there was a flicker of recognition that passed through his gaze.

"Did you see her?" There was an urgency in my voice even though I tried to hide it.

"What do you want with her? Are you with your father?" His questions came out one after the other, the two blending together.

"I am with my father." I quickly looked over my shoulder as if mentioning him would suddenly make him appear. "But I'm not..." I shook my head. "*I* need to find her."

The man's face grew solemn as he met my gaze, the flickering torchlight casting deep shadows across his features. "I won't help you hurt her."

My heart clenched at his words.

"I won't..."

"Rafe. I didn't expect to find you here." My father's voice cut through the tavern, and I turned to see him standing in the doorway, his tall frame blocking out most of the light from outside.

"Davian." Rafe took a small step back, as if he were preparing for a fight. "What are you doing here?"

"You know why we're here." My father took a step into

the tavern, and I could see Reed and Adler waiting just outside the door. "We're looking for the princess."

"Is it true what they say?" Rafe crossed his arms. "About the queen?"

"What is it that they say, exactly?" My father's gaze bore into Rafe, intense and unwavering. His features were tense and guarded, betraying no emotion.

Rafe's eyes darted between my father and me, a mixture of fear and defiance swirling in their depths. "They say she was killed by the rebellion," he finally answered.

My father's jaw clenched. "And the princess? What is it they say about her?"

Rafe hesitated, his gaze flickering toward me briefly before returning to my father.

"They say that you took her."

My father's expression darkened, his jaw working as if he were grinding his teeth. "You know that can't be the truth since you've seen her."

Rafe watched my father, truly studied him. "And you know that I won't help you find the girl who you mean to destroy."

"Destroy?" My father's voice rang out in the dimly lit tavern, a dangerous edge creeping into his tone. "As her father has destroyed our kingdom?"

Rafe stood his ground, his jaw set in determination. "I won't help you. My years of helping you have long since passed. We both know that."

My father's hands clenched into fists as he took a step closer to Rafe, causing the man to straighten his posture in defiance.

"I have my ways to make you help me," my father growled, his voice low and menacing. "You were sworn to serve this rebellion and here you are hidden off in this damned little village." My father stopped once he reached my side. "I haven't had the pleasure of seeing your family yet since we arrived."

Rafe's gaze flickered to me, a silent plea passing between us. He stood firm against my father, his resolve unyielding even in the face of his threats, and it would be a mistake.

My father didn't make empty threats.

"My family has nothing to do with this," Rafe's shoulders were tense and squared, his jaw set. "It's about time you all headed on your way. I think you've overstayed your welcome in this damned little village."

Silence stretched between them, broken only by the faint sounds of the village outside.

"Take him," my father commanded, Reed and Adler stepping through the door just as the order left his lips. "Out back. We'll get the information we need."

Rafe took a step back, but there was nowhere for him to escape as they continued around the bar.

Reed reached out to grab Rafe's arm, but the former ally of my father twisted away, a glint of desperation flashing in his eyes. In one swift motion, he ducked under Reed's outstretched hand and made a dash toward the back door of the tavern.

But he wasn't quick enough, and I clamped my eyes closed as his scream tore through the air.

CHAPTER 6
VERENA

E iran walked closely behind me, his confident strides echoing through the dense forest. His presence at my back was both daunting and comforting. Though I knew I shouldn't have found comfort in him at all.

Eiran had never given me a reason not to trust him, but I couldn't afford to trust anyone at the moment. Not from the rebellion, and not from the palace.

But still, I felt so much safer than being alone.

My steps were heavy, weighed down by everything that was happening. I felt as if I were crossing a burning bridge, one that deserved to crumble and fall. A war ground that left me no choices. My past ripped its claws into me, but my future was so tangled in Dacre, thoughts of him so never-ending that I was suffocating.

All I wanted was to disappear, but the moment I had seen Eiran I realized that maybe all I ever really wanted was to be found.

But when I looked up at Eiran, I still felt lost.

"Right up there." He pointed toward the base of the cliff where a small, shadowy opening sat. The rocks around it were rough and weathered, molded by centuries of wind and water. A faint musty smell emanated from within as we stood at the brink of the opening.

Eiran strode forward with purpose, his hand lifting toward the sky before producing a soft, ethereal glow from his fingertips. The light spilled out in front of us, revealing the interior of the cave as if it were basking in moonlight.

Despite its small size, there was ample space for us to rest for the night.

And to my surprise, it was empty.

The smooth walls and natural formations seemed to welcome us in, offering a sense of safety tucked in the darkness of the cave.

Eiran's light danced across the surface, revealing hidden crevices and glittering minerals embedded in the rock. We could hear the faint trickle of water somewhere in the distance, adding a melody to the otherwise silent space.

A pang of longing gnawed at my stomach. It was reminiscent of the Enveilorian, a place I shouldn't have yearned for. The hidden city wasn't my home.

But I couldn't stop the ache that crept into my chest as memories of being with Dacre assaulted me.

I stepped farther into the cave and nodded toward Eiran's outstretched hand. "How does that work?"

"My magic?" he asked. His head tilted slightly, considering my question.

I nodded as I watched him rotate his hand until the light was pointed directly up at the ceiling.

He ran his other hand over the back of his neck, a distant look in his eyes as if trying to find the right words. "It works just as any other magic, I suppose."

"Which is?" I asked, feeling suddenly inadequate in my lack of knowledge. I was the heir to the kingdom that thrived on magic, yet it felt as much a stranger to me as the people.

He stared at me as if he was trying to figure out why I was asking, since I had no magic that he knew of. "So, it is true that you possess none."

"Have you ever seen me use it?" A gnawing sense of guilt twisted and churned in my stomach, but I couldn't bring myself to feel remorseful for deceiving him.

As he shook his head, his expression shifted, his jaw clenching and his gaze narrowing so slightly I almost missed it.

"And the people I met at the palace either had low level magic or had a very specific type of magic, mostly healers." I paused, trying not to think about why those were the people I had become the most familiar with. "But I've seen magic within your rebellion that I have never witnessed before."

The admission felt shameful. I had been kept in the dark about the very essence of my birthright.

Eiran took a seat and pressed his back against the hard rock wall before he motioned for me to do the same. I did so without hesitation. My body immediately realized as I sank to the ground, groaning in relief as my weight left my feet.

"The magic throughout this kingdom is vast, but almost all magic is influenced by something else." He laid his hand out in front of him and the light cast a glow upon his face. "This, I got from my mother." He twisted his hand back and forth and the light reflected off the cave walls. "But sometimes magic is simply manipulating the energy that the earth gives us," he said, finally closing his fist, making the light vanish and plunging us into darkness once more.

I nodded, my mind reeling as I tried to understand what he was saying.

"But there are also limits to magic," Eiran continued, turning his head until our eyes met. "Even the strongest magic users can only do so much before it takes a toll on their body and their mind."

"How do you know the limit?" I asked, desperate for any kind of understanding.

"Sometimes, you don't." His eyes scanned over my face. "But that's why we train so hard. We need a balance of strength and control."

"Control."

Eiran nodded slowly, his expression grave as he spoke.

"Control is the hardest part of magic. My parents' powers were intertwined and connected. They could sense when the other was losing that control."

I had never heard this before, the idea of two people being so deeply connected through their magic. It was both fascinating and daunting. "Do all marriages have this connection of magic?"

"No." Eiran shook his head. "It's rare. My parents were true mates."

Mates.

It had been years since I had heard that term, not since my mother used to read fairy tales to me as a child. Back then, the concept of mates had seemed as fantastical as dragons and unicorns.

But thoughts of my own magic crept into my mind, of how I hadn't felt a flicker of it since I left Dacre, of how I hadn't been able to find it until I found him.

But just as quickly as the thought entered my mind, I pushed it away.

"What about Dacre's magic?" The question escaped from my lips before I could think twice, and I watched as Eiran's normally soft features hardened in response.

"Why do you care about his magic when he doesn't care about you?" The weight of Eiran's words hit me like a physical blow, causing me to flinch. His sharp tone cut through my defenses, exposing a truth that I couldn't deny.

My fists clenched at my sides as I tried to keep my emotions in check. "He's searching for me just as the rest of the rebellion is, is he not? I would assume that he is far angrier with me than the rest," I retorted through gritted teeth.

I hated that Eiran's words were so capable of slicing open one of my deepest insecurities.

"I'm sorry. You're right," he said sincerely, his voice laced with remorse.

"Why do you hate him so much?" I asked, unable to hide the curiosity and concern in my tone.

Eiran's eyes narrowed, and his jaw clenched before he responded. "Because he's reckless. He lets his emotions cloud his judgment."

"Yet you trusted me," I said, feeling drained. "You should have never trusted me either."

I should have taken his word for the truth, but there was a tinge of envy laced in his tone. The air around us seemed to shift, becoming charged with unspoken tension.

"Where will you go?" he asked, his question catching me off guard.

"What?"

"To get away from here." He waved his hand around the cave. "Why were you in the hidden city to start with? Were you sent there by your father or—"

"I wasn't sent by my father," I interrupted him.

"So going back to the palace isn't an option."

"It's not an option." Memories of the moments that led to my escape flooded my mind, and I instinctively pulled my knees up to my chest, trying to shield myself from them.

"Can I ask why?" He asked the question so softly, so delicately, but still, it made my spine straighten and reignited my urge to run.

"There is nothing left for me in that palace." There hadn't been for a long time.

He hesitated before speaking, his voice filled with a mix of concern and determination. "You can't return to the palace or the hidden city now that Davian knows who you really are. So, what's your plan?"

"Head as far south as I can get. To the Southern Sea." I looked over at him, and I allowed myself to imagine what it would look like. The palace sat on the coast of the Northern Sea, so close that I had grown up feeling the salty air through my window, longing for the freedom and escape that the sea promised. I had watched the waves crash against the sand from my gilded cage, and prayed to the gods that one day that would carry me away with them. "I'm not safe as long as my father can get his hands on me."

"You're his heir," Eiran stated, his voice filled with hesitation and unspoken curiosity. His eyes examined my face, searching for answers to the million questions I could see spinning through his mind.

"You all refer to him as the cruel king. Is it so difficult to believe that he doesn't reserve his wrath only for those who oppose him? My father expects obedience from everyone, and having an heir with no power is seen by him as the ultimate act of disobedience."

I saw him flinch in the darkness, even though he tried to hide it as he attempted to make sense of my words. "I can help you, but we need to be cautious. The rebellion has eyes everywhere."

"And my father?"

"The king has offered a reward for your safe return, which means that anyone who doesn't have a strong loyalty to either side will pick his."

"Because they fear him?"

"Because they are starving. They would do anything for a chance at that reward money, even betray someone they loved. The decision to turn you in would be effortless for them."

I had always known my father was ruthless, careless, but it was hard to hear how desperate the situation had become.

The damp chill of the cave and Eiran's words seemed to seep into my bones despite my efforts to ward them off as I crossed my arms.

"What will the others do when they find out you're helping me?"

His jaw tensed and his gaze turned distant. "I pray they never find out," he replied, his voice strained with emotion.

I gave a silent nod, my chest constricting with each word he spoke.

"You should sleep. I'll take the first watch." Eiran's voice rumbled through the stillness of the cave.

Exhaustion weighed heavy on my shoulders, but I couldn't fight the anxious thoughts swirling in my mind. The ground was hard and unforgiving beneath me as I lay down, using my arms as a makeshift pillow.

As Eiran settled into his position to keep watch, I tried to force myself to relax. But with him here, my mind only raced with more questions and doubts. I clamped my eyes closed and willed sleep to come.

The silence of the cave was broken by every little sound: a rustle in the bushes, the scratching of small animals. Each one caused my eyes to snap open and my heart to race in fear. I curled up tighter, trying to protect myself from the cold night air that seemed to permeate through my skin.

I drifted in and out of consciousness, never able to fully surrender to sleep. Every time I was on the verge of slipping away, a loud noise would startle me back awake. My heart pounded in my chest, ready to flee at any sign of danger. The refuge of the cave now felt like a trap, and I longed for daylight to chase away the shadows and fears.

I sat up, frantically whispering Eiran's name, and I searched the darkness of the cave for any sign of his presence. My heart pounded in my chest as I tried not to alert any potential threats that may have been lurking outside.

"It's just an animal," came Eiran's calm reply from where he was now crouched at the entrance. Relief flooded through me, washing away the fear and tension that had gripped me. "Go back to sleep." He added, "You've barely gotten any rest."

"I'm trying," I replied, attempting to steady my breathing.

Even though I couldn't make out his features in the dim light, Eiran turned to look back at me. We stayed like that for a long moment before he rose and approached me once again. This time, he sat much closer than before, our sides pressed together.

"You're freezing." His words surprised me, and I met his gaze. Slowly, he lowered himself onto his back and tucked his arm beneath my shoulders.

"Come here," he said softly, pulling me close. It felt

wrong to be in his arms, thoughts of Dacre drifting into my tired mind, but his warmth was comforting. As he wrapped his arm around me, my eyes fluttered shut and sleep finally claimed me.

CHAPTER 7
DACRE

"D on't touch me." She took a step back, and my fingers slipped away from her skin.

"Nyra."

"That's not my name." Another step back. *Why was she running from me?*

"That's the name you gave me, remember, little traitor?" I tilted my head and studied her, captivated by the brewing storm in her eyes. Shades of brown and blue swirled together within her irises. It was as if I was being pulled under by her, lost in the depths of her tempestuous beauty. In that moment, I had no desire to come up for air, content to drown in her.

But she refused.

"Did your father send you here?" She looked over her shoulder as if she expected him to appear out of thin air.

"No." I shook my head, trying to clear the fog that seemed to have settled in my mind.

"You're just like him." With each word, she took another step back, creating distance between us. It felt like an invisible barrier had been erected, preventing me from reaching her.

"I'm nothing like him."

She let out a hollow laugh, the sound filled with both sadness and bitterness.

"We are two threads torn from the same cloth." Turning to face me fully, she met my gaze, and I could see the reflection of my own sadness in her eyes.

"Our fathers were one and the same. Two monsters starving for power, and we were built by them to become a weapon. Me for the monarchy and you to take me down."

I shook my head even though she was right. It was exactly what we were raised to be.

Birthed to be enemies.

But in another world, another time, we could have been different.

We could have been more.

We could have been Dacre and Verena.

Instead of the rebel and the heir.

But as she took another step back, thick tendrils of black smoke coiled around her legs like a serpent, encompassing her in its embrace.

"Verena." I reached out for her, calling out her name in a desperate plea to pull her back to me.

But it was no use. The world seemed to be tearing us apart, shredding us at its very seams. No matter how hard I tried, I couldn't bridge the gap between us.

I could feel the grip of the smoke on my skin, threatening to drag me down with it.

"Verena, wait!" I cried out, clawing at the suffocating darkness that clung to me like a second skin.

But my efforts were futile. No amount of fighting could alter our fate.

"I'm sorry," she whispered, barely visible through the thick shroud of smoke that surrounded her and threatened to engulf us both.

But I heard her final plea before she vanished completely.

"Don't become him, Dacre."

I jolted upright, my heart pounding in my chest as I scanned the darkness around me. The sun had long since set, and a blanket of night had descended upon the land, enveloping us in its inky embrace. My eyes strained to pierce through the thick veil of darkness, searching for any glimmer of light.

I rubbed my hand over my face, willing sleep to stop clouding my mind, willing myself to stop thinking of *her*.

But no matter how hard I tried, she was there. Constantly, continually.

I rose from the hard ground, the remnants of the dream still clinging to my mind like cobwebs refusing to be brushed away.

I followed the faint scent of smoke that wafted through the trees. My father was keeping watch when I drifted off to sleep, and as I got closer, I could still see his silhouette outlined against the star-speckled sky as he sat by the small fire.

But he was no longer alone.

I took a deep breath, attempting to steady my nerves that felt frayed from the dream.

"We have to find her before the tithe or we'll be walking into a massacre." The urgency in my father's voice was palpable as he spoke, his words piercing through the quiet of the forest. As I cautiously moved closer, careful to avoid snapping any twigs under my feet, I saw Reed nod in agreement.

"What do you think he'd be willing to sacrifice to get her back?" Reed's voice was low, yet it held a sense of desperation. The crackling of the fire threatened to mask their conversation, but I strained to hear every word.

My father let out a heavy sigh, his weariness evident even from a distance. "If the rumors are true, if the Queen and her unborn child are dead, the princess is the only heir. He will do everything within his power to get her back. We must use that to our advantage once we find her."

My jaw clenched at the mere mention of the king, the man who had shaped both Verena and me into the pawns we had become. The very thought of him having her in his grasp sent a frigid shiver down my spine, igniting a fierce determination within me to find her before it was too late.

But I couldn't allow my father to get to her either.

They were two sides of a deadly blade, forged with the same metal and sharpened to perfection. Both were laced with lethal poison, eager to strike and inflict harm upon their enemies.

As I sat by the crackling fire, its flickering light casting dancing shadows across our faces, I watched my father lean in closer, his features etched with grave concern. "We cannot risk a direct confrontation with the king," he murmured, his words barely audible over the popping embers. "Our best chance is catching him off guard, exploiting his weaknesses for our own gain."

Reed's head bobbed with a slow, deliberate rhythm; his eyes locked onto the flickering flames. It was as if he were searching for answers within their fiery depths, seeking out hidden truths and revelations in the dance of light and shadow. "So we draw him out with the princess?"

"It's a gamble, but the king is always present at the tithe, even if he is heavily guarded. We'll offer him his heir in exchange for the reserves."

Reed's expression remained stoic, but I could see the wheels turning in his mind. "And the princess?"

"Dacre is our heir. There can't be two."

"If we do this. There's no going back," he warned, his voice filled with a sense of finality.

"Dacre will not be okay with our plan." Reed's question hung in the air, heavy with unspoken implications. I tensed, waiting for my father's response.

"He's too damn wrapped up in the girl, but he's our best chance at reaching her before it's too late," my father retorted. "I have seen their connection. He will be the reason she decides to come with us willingly."

My anger burned hot within me, fueling my determination to find Verena before anyone else did. He was my own father, my flesh and blood, and he wanted to use me just as he would anyone else.

I knew who he was, knew of his cruelty and ruthless-

ness, and yet somehow the thought of his betrayal made my
stomach churn.

My mother would weep to know what we had become.
My father so easily willing to use her son in the name
of power, and me so willing to betray him for a girl I
shouldn't have cared for.

"But the moment she is in our grasp, we can't trust him
with her." My father leaned back, and my spine straightened, praying that he didn't see me.

Verena was out there, alone and vulnerable, all because
of my foolishness. I had pushed her away, casting her into
the clutches of cruel men who would drain her dry until she
was nothing but a shell.

My heart raced with fear and guilt as I thought about
what horrors she could be facing at this very moment. The
memory of her being engulfed by the thick black smoke
haunted me, driving me forward with the single-minded
determination to find her before anyone else could.

I crept closer, avoiding any loose branches that could
give away my position. The crackling fire masked my footsteps, but I knew my father's keen senses would pick up
even the slightest sound.

As I inched closer, their voices became clearer, snippets
of conversation drifting toward me like leaves caught in a
breeze. I strained to hear every word, every plan they were
making regarding Verena.

He no longer trusted me, and he was smart not to do so.
Not when it came to her.

"We need to find the reserves." My father wrung his
hands together in front of the flames. "I don't know where

he's storing the power from the tithes, but it has to be in that damn palace."

"And if the king isn't willing to give up that power for his heir?" Reed turned his head and looked at my father.

"Then we'll take the princess back to the hidden city and make her talk. If she doesn't have the information we need, then we'll send a piece of his heir back to him until he sees reason."

My heart hammered relentlessly in my chest, threatening to burst through my rib cage as I clenched my fists at my sides.

"We'll meet Eiran at the Southern Sea. Once we have the heir, we'll lure him out."

Eiran.

That fucking liar. When I asked my father about Eiran's whereabouts, there was no hesitation in his lie that he had returned to the hidden city, but he had sent him after her.

He was keeping me with him because he no longer trusted me, yet he had sent him after her.

Anger and betrayal coursed through me like a raging wildfire, but underneath it all was a fierce protectiveness for her. The mere thought of Eiran hurting her ignited a primal instinct within me, like a rabid animal.

They may not have thought she was mine to protect anymore, but they were fucking wrong.

She was mine. Even if she was running, she was still mine.

I needed to find Verena, away from the clutches of both my father and Reed. She was out there, and I would be the one to find her.

And if Eiran already had, I didn't know what I would do.

As they callously debated their next move, I made a decision of my own. With a silent resolve, I turned my back to them both and disappeared into the darkness of the night before either of them could notice that I was gone.

CHAPTER 8
VERENA

L oose rocks slipped under my feet as we moved down the incline. I glanced over at Eiran, who was leading the way with ease, his agile movements a sharp contrast to my clumsy ones.

He seemed at home, navigating seamlessly through the terrain with sure-footed grace.

I, on the other hand, stumbled and tripped more times than I could count, and was grateful for Eiran's steadying hand when I nearly fell.

We continued in silence for what felt like hours until finally reaching the bottom of the hill. The muscles in my thighs were screaming at me to stop, but I didn't dare mention the thought to Eiran.

We needed to get as far south as quickly as possible, and that was what we were doing. I could rest as soon as I boarded a ship out of this kingdom.

Eiran stopped abruptly, the crunch of leaves and twigs

under his feet coming to a sudden halt. His eyes locked onto mine, his dark brows furrowing. "We need food."

"Okay." I nodded, feeling a familiar ache in the pit of my stomach at his words.

He looked away from me, his gaze lingering on the bow and single arrow that were securely strapped to my back.

"I haven't been able to get anything." Feeling a little foolish that I carried a weapon with me that I hardly knew how to use, I shrugged in defeat.

"May I?" He nodded to the bow. The logical answer was yes, but there was a spike of fear shot through me at the thought of handing over one of my only means of protection.

With hesitant fingers, I unstrapped the bow from my back and passed it to him. He accepted it with a gracious nod, his hand caressing the smooth wood and taut string with a practiced touch.

But as he examined my weapon, all I could think about was the small but deadly dagger tucked into my boot.

My heart raced as I watched Eiran's fingers trace the intricate curves and notches of the bow, his touch reverent and familiar. I couldn't help but feel a sense of unease as I watched him notch the arrow with ease.

His form was flawless as he drew back the string, muscles taut and focused. With a deliberate release, the arrow flew through the air in a graceful arc before piercing into a nearby tree with a satisfying thud.

"That will do." With a swift motion, he moved forward and plucked the arrow from the tree, his muscles rippling under the strain. He turned back to me, and I felt his eyes on me, heavy and intense, causing me to swallow hard as I met his gaze.

"The creek runs just a few feet east." He pointed with the tip of the arrow. "Can you start a small fire while I hunt?"

"Of course," I replied with a nod.

"Keep it small," he cautioned. "We don't want the smoke to draw anyone to us."

Eiran slipped effortlessly into the shadows of the forest, his movements purposeful as he blended with the surroundings. I watched him until he disappeared from view.

He held not only my trust but also my fate in a delicate balance. I prayed that he wasn't careless with either.

I busied myself gathering twigs and leaves. The brittle branches snapped under my fingers as I methodically placed them together, creating a small pile of kindling.

As the flames licked hungrily at their prey, casting a warm glow around me, I couldn't help but feel grateful toward Eiran while simultaneously fighting the urge to run.

I knew that my survival heavily depended on him for the moment, but trust was a luxury that I couldn't afford. Betrayal lurked around every corner, coiled like a venomous snake, waiting for the perfect opportunity to strike. I could feel its presence like a heavy weight on my shoulders, an ever-present reminder of the dangers that surrounded me. Every shadow seemed to hold a secret; every whisper sounded like a warning.

The crackling of the fire soothed my nerves slightly, the warmth a comforting contrast to the fear gnawing at my gut. I couldn't afford to let my guard down. Too much was at stake.

As time dragged on, the forest grew eerily quiet around me, broken only by the occasional rustle of leaves or distant call of a bird. Eiran had yet to return from his hunt, and each passing moment felt heavier than the last.

An unsettling feeling crept over me as I peered into the trees beyond the reach of the fire's light. Shadows seemed to twist and contort, playing tricks on my eyes and imagination. Every rustle of leaves or snap of twigs sent my heart pounding in my chest, my senses on high alert for any potential danger lurking in the shadows.

I tried to focus on tending to the small fire, adding more twigs and dry leaves to keep it burning steadily, but my mind kept drifting back to Eiran and his prolonged absence. *Where was he?*

Doubt and fear gnawed at me, threatening to unravel the thin threads of hope that had been keeping me afloat.

Just as I was about to give in to the panic threatening to consume me, a rustling in the underbrush caught my attention. I tensed, readying myself for whatever—whoever— emerged from the shadows. My hand instinctively went to the hilt of my dagger, my heart hammering in my chest as I braced for the worst.

I was just about to stand when I heard the telltale sound of an arrow releasing from a bow, and swallowed down the scream as a rabbit jumped from beneath the bushes and an arrow met it in midair.

Eiran emerged from the cover of trees, his movements

fluid and sure as he retrieved the rabbit from where it had fallen. He approached the firelight with a small smile, the glow dancing in his eyes as he held up his prize for me to see.

"Dinner," he announced simply, his expression unreadable.

Relief flooded through me at the sight of him unharmed, mingled with a sense of gratitude for his successful hunt. I watched as he expertly cleaned and prepared the rabbit, his hands moving with practiced efficiency while I remained by the fire, readying makeshift skewers for cooking.

His hands were covered in blood, and my stomach lurched at the sight. But my hunger didn't care.

He stood, scrubbing his hands off in the creek, before splashing water on his face.

I skewered the rabbit meat as quickly as I could and almost burned my fingers placing it over the fire.

The scent of roasting rabbit quickly filled the air, mixing with the crackling of the fire as the meat slowly cooked over the flames.

Eiran returned to my side and worked in silence, his focus unwavering as he tended to the meal that would sustain us through the night and probably a few more days to come.

I watched him, the flickering light casting shadows across his face, accentuating the hard lines and angles of his features. There was a ruggedness to him that I found both intimidating and oddly captivating, a duality that kept me questioning who he really was.

He was so different than Dacre. Softness where Dacre had been unyielding. Kind when Dacre had been cruel.

As the rabbit cooked, Eiran glanced over at me and gestured toward a nearby log. "Sit," he said gruffly, his voice soft yet commanding. I obeyed wordlessly, perching myself on the wood as I watched him finish preparing our meal.

He handed me a skewer of cooked rabbit, the scent of the meat making my mouth water. I took it gratefully, trying to ignore the way my gut twisted in hunger.

Eiran settled himself on a log beside me, his gaze distant as he stared into the flickering flames. The crackling of the fire seemed to fill the silence between us as the sun fell lower in the sky.

I tore into the rabbit with my hands and groaned when the warm, savory flavor hit my tongue. The rabbit was small, and there wasn't much meat to share, but it felt like a feast.

We ate in silence, the warmth of the flames chased away the growing chill in the air.

As we finished eating, Eiran wiped his mouth with the back of his hand, his gaze fixed on the dwindling fire. I could see the weariness etched into his features, the weight of our journey pressing down on him like a heavy burden.

"Should you turn back?" I gestured toward the direction we had come from.

"What?" Eiran's gaze flicked over to me, his eyes narrowing slightly as he considered my question.

"Turn back." I fidgeted with my hands, trying to steady

them as I spoke. "You've brought me far enough that I can make it on my own."

When he spoke again, his voice was low and measured. "Turning back is not an option. We must press forward until we get you safely away from this place."

I nodded, though uncertainty gnawed at me. "And what of your safety?"

"What of it?" Eiran's response was curt, as he stared into the dying embers of the fire.

"Do you really think you'll be safe when they find out that you helped me? Do you really think you can keep it from them?"

Eiran's shoulders tensed at my words, a flicker of emotion crossing his face before he schooled his features. He met my gaze, his eyes comforting in the dim light of the dying fire.

"They won't find out," he said, his voice tight with resolve. "They have no reason to think that I'd help you."

Because why would he? Why would Eiran want to help me?

"But what if they do find out?" I pressed, unable to shake off the doubt that clawed at my insides. "What then?"

Eiran's jaw tensed as he considered my question, his silence stretching between us like a taut thread on the verge of snapping. Finally, he spoke, his voice low and tinged with a hint of resignation. "If they find out, then I will deal with the consequences. But until that time comes, we must focus on getting you to safety."

I nodded, but there was still something gnawing at my gut.

"How did you get out without them knowing? Where do they think you are?"

"The entire rebellion is looking for you, Verena. They assume that I am simply doing the same."

His words hung in the air between us, heavy with unspoken truths and uncertainties that lingered beneath the surface. He was putting himself at risk to help me, and I couldn't understand why.

"Tell me something about you."

"What?" His gaze flicked from my eyes to my lips before reaching my eyes again.

"I feel like I barely know anything about you," I answered honestly. "Tell me something. Anything."

A moment of silence stretched between us before he finally broke it with a voice that was surprisingly gentle. "There isn't much to tell," he began, his gaze darting away briefly before returning to me. "The rebellion is all I've ever known. I grew up in the hidden city. It's my home."

"And your mother?" I asked a question I probably shouldn't have, but I had never heard him speak of her before.

Eiran's expression darkened at the mention of his mother, a shadow passing over his features before he composed himself. "She died when I was young."

His voice quivered with a hidden agony, a rawness that spoke of old wounds left unattended. I could feel the pain seeping through his words, a deep hurt that had never fully healed. My heart ached for him, and I longed to offer some form of comfort, but I knew all too well the intensity of that wound.

No matter how hard I tried to move on, the wound in my heart refused to heal. It would scab over, an impenetrable barrier at first glance, but with every small movement, it would crack and break apart. Just when I thought it was finally starting to mend, something would come along and rip it wide open again.

"I'm sorry," I murmured softly because there was nothing else that I could say.

Eiran's eyes narrowed slightly, and his lips formed a tight line. He shook his head slowly, the muscles in his jaw flexing. "It was a long time ago. I barely even knew her."

"That doesn't make it any easier."

Eiran fell silent at my words, his gaze distant as he stared out into the distance.

"Do you look like her?"

A small smile formed on his lips and his eyes finally met mine. "I do." He ran his fingers through his hair. "It's where I get my hair and eyes."

The corners of my mouth lifted as I looked at him. "I bet she was beautiful."

He chuckled, his eyes glinting mischievously. "Does that mean you think I'm beautiful?"

A warm rush of color flooded my cheeks at his playful teasing, but I was determined to hide the effect his words had on me. "I never said that," I countered with a casual tone.

Eiran was beautiful. He wasn't Dacre; he didn't affect me the way Dacre did, but he was still beautiful.

Eiran chuckled again, a low rumble that seemed to chase away the heaviness that had settled between us. "But you were certainly thinking it," he teased, the corners of his mouth turned up in a grin.

I rolled my eyes, unable to suppress a smile at his playful demeanor. "You did feed me, so I couldn't be blamed if I was delusional in my thinking right now," I admitted, feeling a warmth blooming in my chest at the easy banter between us.

"Ouch." He pressed his hand against his chest and pretended to be wounded by my words. "And here I was thinking that you were starting to like me."

"I've always liked you, Eiran." My laughter died off into a soft smile.

"But?"

"There is no but." I straightened, and I wished the conversation would have ended there.

"I would have never treated you the way he did." Eiran's smile faded as he mentioned Dacre, his playful demeanor replaced by a solemn expression. He reached out a hand, his fingers brushing against mine in a gentle gesture that sent a shiver down my spine.

I pulled away without thinking.

"You don't know how he treated me." I wiped my hands along my pants. "I'm here because of my own actions."

Why was I defending him?

"Everyone saw the way he was treating you. It was all anyone could talk about after you ran." His jaw ticked, and he looked away from me. "I would have never hurt you the way he did."

I was paralyzed by the feeling of suffocation, as if

someone were slowly tightening their grip around my neck. *Did he know? Did Dacre tell them what he had done?*

"What?" I barely breathed out the question.

"Dacre's father told him who you really were, and what did he do?" Eiran clenched his jaw so tightly that I could see the muscles in his jaw twitching. "He threw you out of the hidden city as if you meant nothing. The entire rebellion knows that he let you go."

He had done far worse than that. He had used me then sent me on the run as if I could survive the hunt.

But he hadn't taken me to his father.

"I'm tired." I stood quickly and brushed the dirt from my clothing. "We need to keep moving before I lose all my energy."

"Of course." Eiran stood before stomping out the last burning embers of the fire.

CHAPTER 9
DACRE

My legs felt like lead as I trudged forward, each step a struggle.

The weight of my father's disappointment hung heavily on my shoulders. I prayed I had made it deep enough into the forest by the time they realized I was gone, but the thought of his seething fury was nothing compared to thoughts of her.

My father already didn't trust me, and now I had given him even more reason not to.

I had already chosen Verena over him, over the rebellion, when I had let her run instead of bringing her to him, but now, I was choosing her over *everything*.

I knew that he would be furious, but I couldn't find it in myself to regret my decision. Even if that meant that I would pay the consequences when I returned. *If I returned.*

The fear of being caught by them, of them stopping me

from getting to her, consumed me, pushing me onward without pause.

My muscles ached and burned with a desperate need to reach her before they did—before Eiran did.

Time was slipping away, and I could feel the urgency building inside me like a ticking time bomb. I had to get to her.

The only way to do that was to push myself beyond my limits, ignoring the throbbing exhaustion in my limbs and the breathlessness in my chest.

I had already used my magic once to heal myself after I stumbled down the rocky slope, barely managing to stay on my feet as my foot caught on a jutting rock and sent me careening forward.

The jagged edges tore through the skin of my shins, leaving behind deep cuts that stung with every step I took.

My body was already drained from the lack of rest, and the use of my magic to help myself only pushed me further into exhaustion.

In this world, everything came at a price; even our magic had its own toll. I couldn't shake the fear that Verena's price would be the greatest of all.

My gaze lifted up to the bright, full moon above. The sky was painted with midnight blues and purples, and a gentle breeze carried a chill through the air. Determination fueled my steps as I pressed forward, heading toward the southernmost point I could reach.

Eiran was headed to the Southern Sea, and I was almost certain that Verena would be as well. She had told me once that she had dreamed of boarding a boat and sailing away from the life she knew, from the world that set out to destroy her.

But I hadn't realized then how real that dream would need to become.

If Verena was to survive, if she were to have any life worth living, then she had to leave this kingdom behind.

My heart raced as I allowed myself to think of this kingdom without her in it. I had known of the princess all my life, known the role I would play in taking away her crown, and yet, the moment she came into my life, she became it.

I didn't care about her crown, her rule, or the damned king and what he'd be willing to give up for her.

I cared about her, and that was dangerous.

The gentle breeze whispered through the trees, rustling their leaves and sending a shiver down my spine. I rubbed my hands up and down my arms, trying to ward off the chill in the air.

But it didn't work.

The crisp bite of the air was more than just the fall of night. It carried an eerie stillness, as if something was amiss. The hairs on the back of my neck rose, and I couldn't shake the feeling that something lurked just out of sight. A sense of unease settled in the pit of my stomach, warning me to be on guard for whatever was to come.

My senses were on high alert, my power tingling and pulsing in anticipation. My grip tightened on the handle of my dagger, knuckles turning white from the pressure, while my eyes darted back and forth, searching for any movement or threat.

The surrounding woods were still and quiet, but I couldn't stop the unsettling feeling that gnawed at me.

I crouched behind a gnarled oak tree, its twisted branches providing some cover. The rough bark scraped against my palms, but I paid it no mind as I strained my ears. Other than the gentle breeze and the rustling of leaves, there was nothing but eerie silence.

The forest itself seemed to hold its breath, as if even nature knew something was amiss.

What was it?

The minutes crept by, each one leaving a trail of chill bumps on my arms. My hands trembled as I forced myself back to my feet.

My whole body prickled with unease.

I pushed forward, heading deeper south. With each step, my eyes flicked nervously from side to side, scanning every inch of my surroundings. The brittle crunch of leaves underfoot echoed in the stillness of the dense forest.

Every muscle in my body tensed, ready to react, as I trudged on, the unforgiving terrain sapping my strength. But my gut told me not to stop.

My throat was parched, my legs were aching, and my mind felt like it was slowly unraveling. I couldn't tell if it was just figments of my exhaustion, but one thing was for sure, the gnawing feeling in my gut was becoming unbearable, and I knew I needed to find water and rest before continuing on.

I turned toward the west, heading back to the small river I had left behind. I had deliberately stayed a mile away from it, knowing that my father would most likely be near its banks. I followed the familiar path that traced the water's winding journey through our kingdom, longing for a drink.

As I trudged along, my mind raced with a plan. I needed to drink water and find some shelter for a few hours of rest. But my main objective was to reach the south as quickly as possible.

Thoughts of her consumed me.

Go south.

Find her.

And I would. The unknown stretched out before us, a future filled with uncertainties and dangers, but the one thing I knew for sure was, I wouldn't stop until I found her.

A surge of determination flooded me as the river finally came into view.

She was mine, and I would find her.

As that thought solidified in my mind, the hair on the back of my neck stood at attention.

Someone was here.

I cautiously crept closer to the water's edge, my feet softly crunching on the rocks beneath them. The moonlight glinted off the surface of the waters, casting dancing shadows on the rocky bank.

And then, out of nowhere, a voice drifted through the stillness of the night.

"Don't drink so much at once. You'll make yourself sick." The warning was laced with laughter, the sound so familiar I would never be able to forget it.

Eiran.

Silently, I maneuvered closer, my feet sinking into the rocks that crunched softly under my weight. Hiding behind a towering maple tree, I peered around its trunk trying to catch a glimpse of him.

His broad back was turned toward me, completely oblivious to my presence.

He had traveled back to the hidden city.

That was what my father had told me, and even though I already knew he lied, seeing Eiran in front of me just wedged the dagger of my father's deceit further into my chest.

Eiran was here, and he wasn't alone.

"I understand that traveling farther away from the water is smarter to keep us hidden, but gods, am I thirsty."

A chill ran through my veins as I heard her voice.

Verena.

He had her.

I crouched low, my eyes scanning past him until I finally caught sight of her. She was kneeling by the water's edge, her clothing stained with mud from days of travel. Her hair was braided tightly against her scalp, strands of warm brown escaping to frame her delicate features. She cupped water in her hands and brought it to her lips, drinking as if she hadn't had water in days.

Eiran had her, but she was alive and seemingly unharmed.

"I know, but we're gonna make camp for the night soon." Eiran stood with his arms crossed over his chest, his gaze fixed on Verena. "We'll stay nearby, and you can have your fill. I promise."

Verena scooped up another handful of the crystal-clear water and brought it to her lips, taking a long drink before letting the remaining drops fall from her fingers back into the calm current.

Her face was flushed with color and her hair spilled messily around her face, making her seem wild and untamed.

"You're taking first watch this time." She looked up at him as she rose to her feet, and I could see her wince slightly and limp as she shifted her weight onto her injured leg.

She was hurt.

"I'll do whatever it takes to get you off that ankle for a little bit." Eiran nodded, gesturing toward her lower body. "Let's find somewhere safe so you can get some rest."

Verena nodded, her head moving slowly and wearily. Eiran approached her, his steps deliberate as he moved closer. He wrapped an arm around her waist and she leaned into him, trusting him. She draped her arm over his shoulder, clutching his shirt with a white-knuckle grip.

As she shifted her weight onto him, I felt my fists clench at my sides, fighting the urge to rip her away from him.

I hadn't trusted Eiran for as long as I could remember, and I hated that I was right about who he had become. He was the embodiment of our fathers' puppet, his every move controlled by the twisted strings of power.

He used to be my closest friend, outside of Kai, but now he was nothing more than a traitor.

And he was certainly no friend to Verena.

Even if the way he was looking down at her would convince even someone who knew the truth of why he was here that he cared for her.

I hadn't been a friend to her either.

But *fuck*, that was different.

We were different.

Verena…she meant something to me and watching her now with him made my chest ache.

Eiran was consumed by his own desires and the relentless pursuit of this rebellion. He had no regard for anything that didn't align with what they wanted.

And Verena was not safe as long as she was with him.

Every fiber of my being screamed against it, knowing he would only bring her harm.

It didn't matter that he looked down at her so tenderly; he would not be loyal to anyone but the rebellion.

I followed closely behind as they slowly made their way back from the water's edge. Eiran had his hand resting gently on her waist, guiding and supporting her with each step. Her body instinctively leaned into his, fitting against him as she found solace in his presence.

She was comfortable with him.

He had made her comfortable with him.

And somehow that thought was more of a betrayal than anything else.

But for the moment, she was safe and relatively unharmed, and I was here.

My father hadn't been able to get his hands on her, despite his henchman who now had his arm wrapped around her, and neither had the king.

And now that I had found her, I would make sure that they wouldn't be able to.

My mind raced as I desperately searched for a plan to get her away from Eiran, away from them all.

But she didn't trust me.

If she was forced to make a choice between me and Eiran, I feared that I would not be the one she chose.

The weight of this realization suffocated me with its significance.

The sound of her laughter rang through the air, and I watched as she looked up at him, her cheeks dimpled with a smile. He smiled down at her as well, his gaze roaming over the details of her face, and it made me want to break his jaw.

She had betrayed me, and gods, I knew I had betrayed her too. I had been fucking cruel to her out of my own hurt, but none of those things made it any less true that she was still *mine.*

She was the heir to the kingdom, the princess to the fucking king who killed my mother, but none of that made her any less *mine.*

They paused and Eiran gently guided her to a nearby tree, its twisted roots snaking in and out of the ground. She sank down onto the cool earth, leaning back against the bark and stretching out her legs in front of her.

"I need to get this ankle rebraced," Eiran said, his fingers tracing the stitching on her worn leather boots, and I clenched my jaw so tightly that I feared I would crack my teeth.

If it were me, I would heal her, but Eiran did not possess that ability.

My mother used to say that only those who were innately good could heal, and as a boy, I had believed her words when she ran her fingers through my hair and taught me how to fix a scrape on Wren's knee.

But as an adult, I no longer held on to that belief.

It had been hard to see goodness in the world since she died. Impossible to see the good in myself.

I hadn't been able to heal my mother, hadn't been able to save her.

And I hadn't healed anyone else since that day in the palace.

Not until I healed *her*.

I was not good.

Because I would do whatever it took to get her back. Even if she didn't want to be, she was mine.

CHAPTER 10
VERENA

E iran's hands had been gentle when he wrapped my injured ankle with strips of fabric from his own shirt. The soft material was warm against my skin, and I had seen the concern in his eyes as he carefully tucked my foot back into my boot, making sure that it wasn't too tight.

It was the same look he had given me when I had clumsily slid down the embankment and twisted my ankle in the first place.

Despite my attempts to hide it, Eiran had been able to sense my discomfort as I gingerly put weight on it. With a deep frown, he had begged me to rest, but we couldn't afford to.

The sharp pain that shot through my calf with each step was already causing our pace to be much slower than we could allow.

I sprawled out on my back, the blades of rough grass

prickling my exposed skin as I gazed up at the endless expanse of stars above.

The sheer vastness of the open sky above me made me feel insignificant and completely exposed. My thoughts spiraled into a frenzy as panic consumed me—if we were discovered now, I would have no chance of escape or self-defense.

My only skill had always been running, but here, trapped under the open sky, even that would be impossible.

I struggled to banish thoughts of my father's wrath if his men were to catch me. But as I gazed up at the same stars that adorned the sky above the palace, a shiver ran down my spine.

The stars glimmered like gemstones in the inky darkness, illuminating the forest below with an otherworldly glow.

The cool night air caressed my skin, carrying secrets that only added to my unease. Every rustle of leaves made me jump and scan the shadows for any sign of danger.

A torrent of consuming fear flooded my mind, threatening to drown out any sense of reason or hope. Thoughts of my father plagued me. I had feared he wanted me dead, but now with the queen and his new heir gone, I feared much worse.

I was now the sole remaining heir to his throne, a powerless daughter who he had mercilessly tortured in search of any trace of magic within me. And now that I had discovered my power, I dreaded what he would do when he found out.

But as I strained to feel the hum of magic within me, I

found nothing. It was as if my power had abandoned me the moment I left the hidden city's walls.

The unknown of how he would use me was the true terror, lurking in the shadows and gnawing at my mind. My heart raced and my body trembled at the mere thought of being a pawn in his twisted game. The dark possibilities loomed over me like a suffocating shroud, threatening to consume me whole.

My father ruled with an iron fist, forcing his people, our people, to kneel before him and stretch their trembling hands out over a deep well and relinquish a portion of their own magic to him each year.

It was a twisted ritual, one that left them weakened and vulnerable, while he only grew stronger and more formidable.

They were powerless against his tyrannical rule, constantly living in fear of his wrath. The tithe he collected served as a reserve, a safety net that he continued to hoard, and the rise of the rebellion only made his desire for more power insatiable.

His grip on power was unrelenting, making him an unstoppable force to be reckoned with.

I had never seen the reserve of power, never attending the tithe except to watch from my bedroom window, but I knew that it lay somewhere beneath the castle, hidden deep within the tunnels that even my father's enemies couldn't discover.

He had masterfully crafted his rule into a complex labyrinth, confounding any who dared try to unravel its secrets. The very thought of the intricate pathways and secret chambers sent shivers down my spine, for I knew that within them lay my father's true strength and cunning. It was a maze that only he could navigate, a fortress that no one could breach.

The tunnels were a place I had only ventured into a handful of times. The first time was with my mother. I hadn't understood it then, the panic in her voice and the trembling in her hands as she led me down the dimly lit halls until we reached a door that led outside of the palace. I had been so young then, too young, but I hadn't let myself forget that path.

The flames of terror stoked by her panic seared the memory into my mind, leaving an indelible mark.

The other times, I had been with my father and his men. I could still hear the echoes of screams and cries ringing through the dark, damp walls. My father believed he was training me, grooming me to be a queen with no mercy or empathy. A queen who learned to take what she needed from her people by any means necessary.

But all he did was teach me how to survive in a world of darkness and cruelty.

Reluctantly, I gave in to the relentless pull of longing I always tried to avoid. My heart ached for my mother, her warm embrace and soothing words that were always able to ease any pain.

I wished that she were still here.

I yearned for the days when I believed that my father loved her, loved me.

But as the stress of me being powerless weighed heavier on him, he slowly became someone else. He withdrew from my mother, from me, and she had become my only shield from his cruelty.

But when she passed, that shelter was taken with her, leaving me vulnerable to his increasing malice.

Her death stole his chance at another heir, and he became consumed by bitterness and rage. It felt like a part of him had been buried in the ground beside her.

She had stolen his chance at another heir, taking that heir with her when she died, but it also cast a dark shadow over the entire kingdom, spreading its grip on everyone and everything in its wake.

But despite not being the male heir they desired, a powerful heir, my mother still loved me.

I absently wondered what she would have done if she were still alive. Would she have taken me and fled the king-dom? Or would she have stayed by his side, watching help-lessly as he spiraled into darkness.

Either way, I knew that I never could have stayed and become everything he wanted me to be. It would mean losing all sense of me, becoming a mere husk of the girl I once was.

He had already stripped me of so much, and I refused to let him take any more.

Not him or this damn rebellion that would rather see me dead.

I was a powerless girl in a game crafted by powerful men. They moved their pieces with calculated precision, and I couldn't outmaneuver them.

All I could do was run.

I squeezed my eyes closed, beseeching the gods to grant

me just a few hours of sleep. The weight of exhaustion hung heavily on my bones, threatening to crush me into the ground, and the thought of the rising sun filled me with dread.

We were already taking too many risks by staying here tonight. Both Eiran and I knew it, but he also knew I couldn't go any farther with this cursed ankle slowing me down like an anchor dragging behind me.

I needed rest. We both did.

But as soon as I closed my eyes and tried to clear my mind, my thoughts drifted to Dacre. They constantly drifted to him, like a feather caught in the wind. I couldn't get it to stop.

His stormy eyes, filled with emotion and intensity, pierced through my mind, the memory of his touch.

Where was he?

Was he out there searching for me, consumed by anger and bitterness toward my betrayal? I could only imagine that he was, fueled by his unwavering loyalty to the rebellion.

But I was furious with him as well.

The realization that we had both betrayed each other simmered in me.

I had allowed myself to care for him. Trusted him, and it was a mistake.

Neither of us were born into a world where trust came easily. Suspicion and doubt had lingered between us from the moment we first laid eyes on one another, and I had foolishly let my guard down.

And yet, I still yearned for him.

Despite everything he had done, I couldn't help but long for the man I knew.

Knew—what a twisted irony that word had become. Neither of us truly knew the other.

He thought I was Nyra, the girl from the kingdom who escaped an evil king, but I wasn't that girl. I was Verena, daughter to the queen, pawn to the king who would see our kingdom in ruin.

And I had deceived him. I lied to him over and over, and the weight of that guilt made my skin crawl with each passing moment.

He was right. I was nothing but a traitor.

His actions were fueled by anger toward me, toward what I had done, but that did little to ease the pain and betrayal I felt.

The wounds he'd inflicted were still raw and throbbing, a constant reminder of his cruelty.

A constant reminder that he wasn't here.

A sudden jolt, like a buzz of lightning, ran down my spine, and I snapped my eyes open. I scanned the darkness, searching for any sign of Eiran.

He stood tall by the towering tree, his silhouette blending into the night. His unwavering gaze was fixated on the surrounding forest as he maintained his steady patrol.

As I opened my mouth to call out his name, the familiar tang of magic coated my tongue and traveled down my throat, a pulsing sensation that spread through every inch of my body.

As soon as I stepped out of the hidden city, my power seemed to evaporate into thin air.

But I could feel it now.

The energy that had coursed through me while using magic with Dacre was now a faint echo, like a whisper in a crowded room. The remnants of my power were like a lingering taste in my mouth, teasing and elusive.

It felt like my power was both present and absent at the same time, playing tricks on my mind.

Slowly and carefully, I sat up and took in my surroundings. The moon cast a pale light over the landscape, illuminating the trees and casting deep shadows across the forest floor.

I searched for any signs of disturbance or intrusion, my heart racing with anticipation. But as far as I could see, everything appeared untouched and undisturbed.

The gentle trickle of the nearby river was soothing, but it did little to ease the tension building within me. In the distance, the eerie calls of nocturnal birds echoed through the trees, haunting me as I looked around.

My ears strained for any indication of another presence, but all I could hear was the rapid beating of my own heart. I squinted into the darkness, scanning every inch of the surrounding area. My eyes darted back and forth, trying to catch even the slightest movement in the darkness.

Was someone else here?

The sensation of my magic teased and taunted me, a constant game of fleeting presence and absence. One moment, it surged through my veins like a raging river, but just as quickly, it would dissipate like mist in the wind, leaving me feeling empty and longing for its return.

And yet, just as suddenly, it would reappear, coursing through every inch of my being once more.

What was happening to me?

I glanced over at Eiran, his eyes scanning our surroundings with ease and confidence. While my body was tense with uncertainty, he seemed unbothered by whatever was happening.

I let my gaze drift over his sharp jawline and the relaxed way he held his hands at his sides.

I didn't understand my magic or how it worked, but there was a part of me that feared that the moment I walked away from the hidden city, that Dacre had somehow taken it from me.

After all, I had never possessed any magic until I arrived there, until him.

And the moment I left, it was gone.

But I could feel it now.

The sensation coursed through my veins like a potent drug, leaving me trembling and yearning for more. It was as if I had been deprived of magic my entire life, and now that I had tasted it, I couldn't get enough. My body and mind craved its power, desperate to wield it once again.

I had been powerless my whole life, and that taste of power, it felt dangerous.

I knew my father would stop at nothing to exploit this power for his own gain, but that was only if his men caught me.

I couldn't let them catch me.

Not them nor the rebellion because I feared what either side would do.

Yet, I knew that there had to be a lesser of two evils in this war-torn kingdom.

If Dacre's father got his hands on the reserves, would he use it to help the people of this kingdom like he promised, or would he become just as ruthless as my father?

And what of Dacre himself? Would his loyalty to the rebellion blind him to his father's ruthless ways?

Would Wren's?

I pushed away the tumultuous thoughts and let my gaze linger on Eiran once more. In his presence, I felt a sense of comfort. He had come for me.

Even when his loyalty should have lied elsewhere. Eiran was a rebel. He was meant to be my enemy, but he was still here.

When Dacre discovered my true identity and banished me, Eiran had found me.

As I settled back onto the hard ground and closed my eyes, remnants of magic still trailing through my veins, I tried to force myself not to wish it had been Dacre instead.

CHAPTER 11
VERENA

A deafening clang shattered the stillness of the night, jolting me awake. My heart raced as I frantically scanned our makeshift camp.

The icy chill of the air clawed at my skin, but I ignored it as I searched for any sign of Eiran.

He was gone.

Panic surged through me as I strained to hear any noise over the pounding of my own heart. And then it came—the unmistakable sound of approaching footsteps.

Someone was here, someone had come for me, and I needed to hide before they found me.

I heard it then, the metallic clash of weapons, followed by a pained grunt. Eiran's instructions echoed in my head, determined to protect me at all costs.

When he had told me that if the time ever came, I should run, I didn't know what I would do. But now, with trembling limbs and blurred vision, I made a split-second decision to do just that.

My body was battered and weak, no match for the danger ahead. If I stayed, I would only be a burden to Eiran in any potential fight.

If either of us stood a chance, I couldn't get in his way.

Following Eiran's instructions, I turned and headed east, away from the river's edge.

Head east away from the river then south.

We'd meet at the Southern Sea. That was what he told me.

I had to make it to the Southern Sea.

Each step sent a searing pain shooting through my ankle, the tight fabric Eiran wrapped around it only adding to the discomfort.

But I couldn't stop.

I forced myself to keep moving, picking up speed as much as I could despite the throbbing ache. My eyes scanned the surroundings for any signs of danger as I pushed forward relentlessly.

The forest seemed to close in around me as I sprinted, my heart pounding in my ears. The dense foliage and brush made it difficult to see more than a few yards ahead, but I kept pushing forward.

Suddenly, a soldier dressed in my father's army uniform stepped out from behind a large tree, blocking my path. I skidded to a stop and reached for my dagger, adrenaline coursing through my veins. The soldier's smirk was menacing, and I braced myself for a fight.

"There you are, Princess." As he spoke, the soldier tilted his head to the side, his smirk growing wider. His blond hair fell across his forehead, covering one of his eyes. "The entire kingdom has been looking for you."

My mind raced, trying to come up with a plan. I couldn't let him get too close, but if I were to throw my dagger, I would be left defenseless with no other options.

"What for, exactly?" I asked, trying to buy myself some time. My fingers tightened around the worn handle of my dagger, bracing myself for what would come next.

"To take you back home." His words hung in the air like a thick fog, each syllable carrying a weight that seemed to press down on me. As he closed the distance between us, his scrutinizing gaze roamed over every inch of my body, searching for any sign of vulnerability. "To get you out of the hands of that damned rebellion."

My heart raced as I shifted my stance, trying to hide the pain in my injured leg, but his sharp gaze immediately homed in on my discomfort and I swore under my breath. "As you can see, I'm not in the hands of anyone, and I don't want any trouble."

"It would appear that trouble is exactly what you are, Princess. You're the heir to our kingdom, and yet, here you are, hiding out in the woods with one of those rebels instead of the palace where you belong."

The crunch of leaves underfoot filled the space between us as I took another small step to the right.

"Your father's very eager to get you home, to keep you safe."

Safe.

A snarl of defiance rose in my throat, but I bit it back. Each second spent in that palace put me in danger.

"I have a few more places in our kingdom I'd like to see first." I inched farther from him, my hand clenched around my dagger, and we began to circle each other like two predators stalking their prey. He mirrored each step I took, our eyes trained on one another. "Do you care to let my father know that I'll be home soon?"

My challenge was met with a wide grin and baring teeth that made my stomach turn.

"I'm afraid that's not possible, Princess. You're coming with me today." He wasted no time as he charged toward me, arms outstretched and determination shining in his eyes.

I stumbled backward, my injured ankle slowing me down, but still, I refused to give up.

With every fiber of my being, I tried to outrun him and escape this fate that awaited me.

My breath came in a ragged gasp as I ran, but he was right behind me, his footsteps pounding against the ground like a war drum.

I felt his hand close around my waist, his grip like iron as he pulled me back. My attempts to fight back were futile, my dagger slicing through the air uselessly as he dragged me closer with every step. The impact of my back slamming into his chest knocked the wind out of me, leaving me gasping and vulnerable.

My training in the hidden city deserted me, fear and desperation clouding my thoughts. My body could not match his brute strength and agility. In a moment of pure instinct, I thrashed and clawed at him, crying out at the searing pain as my injured ankle collided with his body.

But he only chuckled darkly, tightening his hold on me and reveling in my struggles.

"Aww, Princess," he taunted as he brushed his nose against the back of my neck, causing me to recoil away from him. "This is no way to treat the man who's saving you."

A shiver of dread shot down my spine as his hot breath brushed against my skin like a sinister caress, igniting a burning sensation that engulfed me in unease. One of his hands tangled into the hair at the base of my skull, and I could feel every hair on my body stand on end, anticipating the next move he would make with a mixture of fear and revulsion.

With a violent jerk, he pulled me back, causing me to let out a piercing scream as a searing pain shot through my head.

"Such a pretty princess." I could feel his lips pressing against my bare neck as if he were inhaling deeply and savoring my scent. It made me feel like an object, something to be possessed and controlled by him.

It made me feel utterly powerless in his hold.

Tears blurred my vision as I desperately tried to pry his fingers from behind my head. My nails dug into his skin, but he refused to release me.

"We're getting you back to the palace today." The soldier's grip on me was tight, his calm voice in stark contrast to my frantic struggles against him. "We're getting you back to the palace, and the king is going to reward me so handsomely for doing so. I am the soldier that saved the princess, that saved the heir. Can you imagine what he'll do?"

The thought made bile rise in my throat.

I wanted to scream and plead for this man to let me go. I didn't care how weak it was. I couldn't go back to the palace. I couldn't go back to my father.

A guttural, primal scream tore from my throat, but it fell on deaf ears as the soldier remained unmoved, his hand tightening on my hair as if to silence me.

"Please," I begged with tears streaming down my face.

A sudden, sharp whistle split through the air, followed by a deep thud that reverberated through my body.

The unmistakable thud of metal against flesh rang out.

The soldier stumbled back, his breath hot and panicked on my skin as he reached for his weapon.

But his other hand remained locked in my hair, wrenching me down with him as he fell. A searing pain shot through my scalp as strands of hair tore away, and I let out a cry as I landed on top of him.

The stench of sweat and blood filled my nostrils as I tried to scramble away from him.

I gasped, horrified by the gruesome sight that met my eyes. A dagger cruelly protruded from his neck, and blood gushed from the wound and his lips, staining the grass beneath him and creating a pool of scarlet around his head.

He gasped for air, his hands frantically clawing at the weapon as if he could somehow stop the bleeding, but it was no use. His fate had been sealed with that fatal blow.

My stomach churned as I spun around, searching frantically for the culprit who had thrown the dagger.

Eiran.

My eyes scanned the area, seeking any sign of movement, but he was nowhere to be seen. Without hesitation, I climbed to my feet and took off in the direction of the weapon's trajectory, my feet pounding against the ground.

South. We were headed south.

Tears and mucus streamed down my face, mixing with the dirt and sweat that coated my skin. I frantically wiped at them, a mixture of determination and terror fueling my movements. Despite the searing pain shooting through my ankle, I pushed forward with a limp, my mind solely focused on reaching Eiran before it was too late.

Each step felt like an eternity as I trudged through the forest, the sound of my own rapid breaths pounding in my ears.

Every rustle of leaves made me jump, fear gripping my heart. If this one soldier was here, there was no telling how many more were with him.

My father, with his endless resources and countless men at his disposal, could have sent an entire army after me, and that one soldier that was dying in the forest behind me wouldn't matter.

He sacrificed his life in the name of a king who would never think of him again.

As I cautiously made my way through the dense thicket, the distant sounds of shouting and grunting grew louder with each step. My hand instinctively reached out to grasp a sturdy tree trunk, its rough bark providing a sense of stability as I carefully surveyed my surroundings, determined to remain hidden from view.

The thick canopy above filtered the dim light of the rising sun, casting dappled shadows over the scene before me. Finally, I could make out Eiran's face in the midst of the chaos. His features were twisted in unbridled rage as he held one of the soldiers off the ground by his collar. The man's body hung limply, completely at Eiran's mercy.

With a snarl, Eiran brought the soldier's face close to his own, their noses almost touching. In his fury, flecks of spit flew from Eiran's mouth with each word that dripped with venom.

"You filthy fucking palace scum," he seethed, his grip on the soldier tightening. "Take this message with you to your gods. Your king that you serve won't be king much longer. Long live the rebellion."

Eiran's movements were swift and fluid as he lifted his dagger and slit the man's throat, causing blood to spray out and splatter on Eiran's face.

But he didn't flinch or shy away; instead, he seemed to revel in the brutal act.

His eyes were wild and frenzied as he wiped the blood from his dagger onto his thigh before turning it over in his hand.

The metallic flint of his blade caught my eye as I stumbled back in shock and confusion. He still held tightly on to the weapon that had just taken a life.

His dagger.

He still had his dagger, but the soldier I left behind still had one protruding from his neck.

Eiran was a man consumed by vengeance and fueled by rebellion, his features contorted with a mixture of madness and triumph.

He looked nothing like the person I had known for the past few days. There was a cruelty dripping from him that reminded me of my father.

I took another step back, needing to put distance between us.

Eiran hadn't thrown that dagger.

A rustling behind me made me spin around, my hand instinctively reaching for the dagger at my belt. But before I could even fully turn, a large figure crashed into me, their hand muffling my scream as they pinned it against my mouth.

I struggled against them, punching and kicking wildly, but they were too strong.

I was dragged back several feet, my vision obscured by the shadows. I struggled to get a clear view of my assailant, their figure towering over me in the dim light. They were much larger and more muscular than the other soldier, and I knew a physical fight would be futile.

Just as Eiran disappeared from my sight, fear and adrenaline coursed through my veins and I mustered all my strength to thrust my dagger backward with all my might. With a satisfying thud, metal met flesh and I knew I had struck my attacker.

"Fuck." The low, guttural curse escaped his lips as his hands slipped away from me.

I whirled around, desperate to escape, only to be stopped by his hand on mine.

Dacre.

He stood before me, breathing heavily and clutching his upper thigh where my dagger was now embedded. My mind raced as I tried to figure out what to do.

His hand clenched tightly around mine, and I yanked it away, heart pounding in my chest like a wild animal trying to escape.

"Don't fucking touch me." I stumbled backward.

His gaze zeroed in on my injured ankle, his dark eyes flitting back and forth between it and my face.

Had he already known?

Memories of the dagger flying past my face and the surge of my magic that had come back to me the night before flooded my mind.

The magic that felt so potent in my veins right now.

He had been here. He was watching me.

I could feel the heat emanating from his body as he got closer, and I instinctively pushed him away with all my might, slamming my hands into his solid chest.

"No!" My voice quivered with rage and fear. "Don't you dare touch me."

"Verena," he said my name with such familiarity, as if he had the right to speak it, as if it was a desperate plea.

And I hated it.

"Don't," I repeated, taking another shaky step back. The space between us felt like an ocean now, but even that distance didn't feel far enough to escape the anger and hurt burning inside me.

But he didn't listen. His hand clamped down over my

mouth once more, muffling any cries or protests I could make.

With unexpected strength, he hoisted me up against his body and I had no chance in a fight against him. Even with a dagger still embedded in his leg—my dagger—he pressed on, his determination etched into every line of his face as we moved south, away from Eiran and my father's men.

He was here, and I felt at peace and on fire all at once.

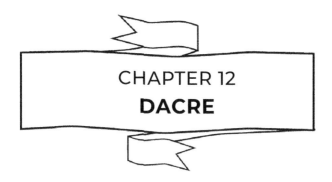

CHAPTER 12
DACRE

My grip tightened around Verena, my fingers digging into her skin as I fought to control my breathing. The heat of Verena's body mixed with my own creating a slick sheen between us, and her heart beating frantically against my chest mirrored the rapid pace of my own.

Every movement she made was like a storm raging inside me, her body tense and resistant in my grip.

The anger that crackled between us was tangible, but I could deal with our anger.

It was the fear that was etched across her features that tore me apart. That fear was a constant reminder of the enemies we both faced, of the enemies we had become.

I could hear it in her gasping breaths, feel it pulse through her body as she trembled against me. I wanted to push it away, to ignore the invisible, suffocating haze that threatened to smother us both.

The distant sound of twigs snapping made my muscles tense and my heart race even faster than it already was. I froze and held my breath, hoping somehow that our stillness would keep us hidden.

Verena's eyes widened with fear as I finally let her feet touch the ground. She opened her mouth to speak, likely to scream at me, but I silenced her with a finger pressed against her lips and the shake of my head.

We both listened as the sound of footsteps grew closer, our hearts pounding in tandem.

For a moment, our gazes locked, and time seemed to stand still. I wanted to drown in her, to beg for her forgiveness, but we didn't have time for that. Not now.

Not when her pupils dilated as they darted back and forth, searching for an escape we both knew was unlikely to be found.

I looked away from her and scanned the forest.

"Stay close to me," I whispered, my voice barely audible over our ragged breaths.

She didn't answer, her eyes fixed on mine with determination and fear mirroring my own.

The sound of approaching footsteps grew louder, sending my heart into a frenzy against my ribs. With a deep breath, I took Verena's hand and guided her deeper into the thicket of trees, their gnarled branches creating an intricate maze around us.

The pain in my thigh was brutal, but I refused to remove the dagger embedded in it. If we stopped now, I risked bleeding out before I could tend to the wound. We had to keep moving, no matter how agonizing each step became.

I led Verena through the dim forest, the trees seeming to swallow everything around us, but the footsteps continued to follow. It was as if they were closing in, the echoes of men coming closer and closer.

I didn't know if they were her father's men or mine, but I didn't care. I refused to allow either one of them to get to us.

"Over here!" The shout pierced through the air, far too close, and jarred us into action.

I gripped Verena's hand and pulled her to the ground, both of us landing with a soft thud. I pressed my body against Verena's, shielding her as I peered through the bushes.

The soldier's footsteps pounded against the forest floor, the leaves and twigs crunching under his heavy boots as we watched him pass. Our own breaths were loud in our ears, the sound of our heartbeats drowning out any other noise.

Verena's body convulsed against mine, her terrified whispers filling the air around us. I wrapped my arms tightly around her, pressing my lips to her ear as I tried to calm her trembling form. "We're okay," I whispered urgently in her ear. "Just breathe. I won't let them touch you."

I leaned back slightly and gazed down into her eyes, searching for any sign that she believed me, that she trusted me.

But all I could see was fear and doubt reflected in them.

Fear and doubt that I had given her.

But she didn't look away. We held each other's gaze for what felt like an eternity, listening intently as the footsteps of the soldiers faded into the distance.

With a heavy sigh of relief, I slowly released my grip on her and eased my body off hers before helping her stand up on shaky legs.

Her hands were entwined with mine, the warmth of her touch sending a rush of power coursing through my body.

In the distance, a lone shout echoed from the west, the sound of footsteps receding behind it. But I refused to release her hand as we began moving forward, heading south.

As the sound of their footsteps faded into the distance, I slowed my pace, wincing when I looked back and saw the pain on Verena's face as she struggled to keep up.

"I need to stop," she gasped, pulling her hand out of mine before bending over and bracing herself on her thighs.

"Let me see." I started to crouch before her, reaching for her wounded leg, but she pushed me away forcefully.

"I told you not to touch me," she snarled, her chest rising and falling rapidly as she backed away from me.

I gritted my teeth, my frustration boiling just below the surface.

"We need to find a place to rest," I said, my voice low and steady, trying to keep any emotion from leaking out. "We need to find somewhere for me to heal you."

But she took a step back, her face contorting with anger and hurt. "We don't need to do anything," she spat, pointing aggressively toward the forest behind us. "You need to leave."

"I'm not going anywhere," I stated firmly, my resolve unshaken.

A bitter laugh escaped her lips, filled with pain. "Why the hell not? Wasn't it you who fucked me then threw me out like the traitor I am?"

Her words were like daggers, but I refused to look away from the emotions burning in her eyes. The pain I saw there, the hurt I caused, made me recoil.

"Verena." I reached out my hand toward her, pleading with her to listen.

But she flinched, avoiding my touch as if I would burn her. Her eyes flashed with anger and resentment, as if my very presence was causing her pain.

"Don't call me that." Her tone was laced with venom and resentment.

"Your name?" I scoffed, feeling a surge of anger bubbling up inside me. I didn't want to be angry with her, but it was like trying to grasp onto fire, volatile and unpredictable.

And I couldn't stop it even though I knew I had been far more cruel to her than she could ever be to me.

"The one you used against me? Yes."

I fought against the urge to lash out, to take my anger and fear and use it to hurt her back, but I felt so volatile when it came to her, so out of control.

"You mean the name that you lied to me about over and over again." My heart clenched at the memory of her betrayal.

"I didn't have a choice," she said through gritted teeth, her hands balled into fists at her sides.

"And you left me no choice," I countered, my voice trembling with all the things I wasn't saying. "What did you expect me to do? My father knew who you really were, he demanded…" I shook my head and tried to push thoughts of my father from my mind.

"I don't give a damn about you or your father." Verena's face was contorted with anger, her eyes narrowed and filled with undisguised hatred. "What was it that he demanded of you, Dacre?"

My name on her lips sent a chill across my skin.

"Did he order his son, his successor, to fuck the lost princess before he threw her out of the only place she had been safe for years?"

"Verena," I called her name again, but she wasn't listening.

She looked behind her at the way we had just come. "I want to go back to Eiran."

A wave of hot, red fury surged through me at the sound of his name on her lips. My hands clenched into fists and my jaw tightened as I forced myself to stay calm.

I had betrayed her, had hurt her, but Eiran would do much worse. "Over my dead body will you go back with him."

"That's not up to you." Her words were like venom, sharp and deadly, and I let out a low growl before taking a step closer to her.

But she didn't back away. Instead, she met my gaze

with defiance, her eyes blazing with a fire that mirrored my own.

"Stay away from me," she warned, her voice so low and so filled with hurt.

"We both betrayed the other, remember." The fight was leaving both of us.

But as her vulnerability slipped through her facade, her voice trembled with hurt. It made me want to crumble before her, despite everything she had done. Everything we both had.

"Then why are you here?" The fire in her eyes dimmed as she searched my face. "Why, Dacre? Do you not think I know what your plans are, apparently what they have been all along? If you want to take the kingdom, then take it. You don't need me to do so."

"Is that why you think I'm here?" My voice was barely audible, barely there.

She stared up at me, her expression inscrutable.

"I think that Eiran found me to help me get away, but you?" She shook her head as she assessed me, her gaze unwavering. "You're as much a pawn to your father as I am to mine. The difference is that I don't want to be."

My heart pounded in my chest, each beat echoing like a drum in my ears. It felt as though I was drowning in her words, suffocating under the weight of their truth. I took a deep breath, trying to steady myself, but it only seemed to smother me more. "I am not here for my father."

"I don't believe you." There was no deceit in her words or the way she was looking at me. If she had ever trusted me before, I had completely torn that away.

"My father plans to use you to lure out the king." I hated how traitorous I felt saying those words. I was betraying my blood, betraying the entire rebellion, and even as pain sliced through my chest, I didn't regret it. "They are going to use you at the tithe, a trade to find the power reserves."

"What?" There was so much fear in Verena's eyes now. "He won't give up those reserves. Not for me, not for anyone."

"I overheard my father and Reed talking. If he doesn't give them up, they plan to torture the information out of you, tear you apart limb from limb and send them back to your father until he relents."

"I don't know where the reserves are. My father, he..." Panic. I could taste her panic on my tongue as if it flooded the very air we breathed.

"Listen to me." My hand reached out to grasp her arm, but she violently jerked away from my touch. Her eyes darted behind her, and I couldn't help but feel a surge of jealousy. "I won't let that happen to you."

She looked back behind her again, and I hated that she was probably looking for him.

"He sent Eiran here to find you." I clenched my teeth, my voice laced with bitterness. "They are planning to meet him at the Southern Sea to take you back."

Verena's piercing gaze met mine, searching for any hint of truth in my words. "Yet it is you who they plan to make king?"

"That's not what I want." The admission tasted like poison on my tongue. It had been my father's plan all along, a plan that I had known since I was a young boy, and I had wanted it until her. But everything was different now. I was different. "Not anymore."

"I don't believe you." She shook her head in disbelief and took another small step away from me.

"Let me heal you," I pleaded, motioning toward her ankle. "I don't need you to trust me, but at least let me heal you."

"My dagger is in your leg.," she stated the obvious, and as if she had summoned it, pain immediately gripped me.

"I will deal with my leg after your ankle is taken care of," I promised, determined to ease her pain.

Her expression hardened, her eyes narrowing on my face. "How long have you been watching me?"

I swallowed hard, feeling a knot form in my throat. "Long enough to know that you need my help."

A brief glimmer of hope shone in her eyes before quickly fading away into a cold wall of mistrust. "What do you want from me?" she demanded, her voice raw with emotion.

"I want to heal you, then I want to get you out of this kingdom," I answered honestly. I couldn't make sense of anything other than those truths.

She took a step back, warily eyeing the surrounding forest before meeting my gaze once again. "I'll never trust you again."

"Good." I nodded. "Don't trust anyone, Verena."

CHAPTER 13
VERENA

Night had already fallen, shrouding the world in a deep indigo hue, and Dacre and I had hardly exchanged more than a handful of words.

He strode ahead of me, leading the way with purposeful strides, and I wanted to scream.

Every step he took was filled with restrained power, his muscles visibly tensing and releasing beneath his shirt. Despite the anger etched into his features, that same anger that stewed inside me, I couldn't tear my eyes away from the way his shirt hugged every bulge and curve of his broad shoulders and back.

And that only fueled my frustration further.

"How much farther to the coast?" I asked, my voice strained as I sought to divert my mind to anything else.

Dacre turned back to me, his expression momentarily startled by my question. "At least another day," he replied, his voice steady but tinged with uncertainty. "Maybe more."

His gaze wandered over me, lingering as it fell to my ankle. "Why? Is your ankle hurting again?"

"No. It's fine." I shook my head, trying to push away the rising feelings in the pit of my stomach.

I had allowed him to heal me, allowed him to touch me, and now my ankle was healed, but my stomach was in knots.

His hand had been too gentle against the back of my calf as he prodded and massaged my injury, just like he had before in the springs. The touch of his fingers had been a caress, a promise of something more that I shouldn't want.

He had branded me a little traitor, but it was my own body that had turned against me. My skin betrayed my pleas to the gods, responding to his touch as if bewitched.

My flesh didn't recall the venomous way he uttered my true name before casting me out of his room, exiling me from his city. Instead, it held on to the ghost of his caress, the way he made promises with his fingers that could never fall across his lips.

Ignoring the pain of my dagger lodged deep in his thigh, he poured his magic into healing my battered body. Sweat beaded on his forehead as he focused every ounce of strength on repairing me.

And I remembered what Eiran had told me.

"Even the strongest magic users can only do so much before it takes a toll on their body and their mind."

With a gasp of relief I watched as my wound healed, leaving nothing but the faintest of bruises in its wake.

Finally, with a shaky hand, he removed the blood-stained dagger and pressed a firm palm against the gaping wound in his thigh. His face contorted in agony as he channeled his power into mending the severed muscles and tendons.

But even as he winced in pain, his gaze roamed over me again, as if checking to make sure that he didn't leave any spot unhealed.

And when he was done, he wiped his blood from my blade and handed back my weapon without fear or hesitation, as if I posed no threat to him.

My fingers trembled as I grasped the familiar weight of my dagger, its sharp blade a comforting reminder of the power I held in my hand.

Without it, I felt utterly vulnerable and powerless.

But even though I had lodged the blade into his flesh, he had given it back.

"We'll need to be careful as we travel closer to the coast. My father and his men will be looking for you and Eiran there, and I'm sure the King's Guards will be as well." He paused for a moment before he spoke again. "He should know that there's nowhere else for you to run."

Why was he here?

The thought flooded my mind, drowning out every other, and leaving me struggling to make sense of it all.

He had pushed me away with such cold indifference, ordering me to run. And now he was guiding us farther south, away from his father's stronghold.

My instincts screamed that this could be a trap, a cunning ploy to capture and control me. Perhaps he had only healed me to gain my trust before leading me straight into their clutches.

My gut churned with turmoil, torn between the need for answers and the lingering ache in my chest that begged me to trust him.

He had done nothing to earn my trust, yet foolishly part of me still clung to it.

I had been hopeful when Eiran found me, desperate for his help, but this was different. There wasn't a single part of me that wanted to trust Dacre.

I wanted to scream and plead with my stubborn heart not to give in, yet it seemed to have a will of its own. It fluttered and ached, torn between logic and emotion.

"We need to stop for the night soon and get some rest." His voice broke through my thoughts, causing me to jump slightly. "We'll have a full day of travel again tomorrow."

But before he could suggest a spot to make camp, I spoke up hastily. "I want to keep going."

My words hung heavy between us, filled with unspoken tension. But the thought of being alone with him in the dark, quiet night put me on edge.

I had been following him on a mission to get somewhere safe, but the moment we stopped...

He stared at me for a moment before slowing down his pace. But I didn't stop walking, determined to put as much distance between us as possible.

"Verena, we need to rest," he called out after me, his voice filled with concern.

But I didn't stop, unwilling to give in to his demands,

and the sound of his footsteps getting closer only fueled my determination.

"Maybe you do, but I want to keep going."

"Do you always act this foolish?" His words were sharp and laced with frustration, causing a shiver to run down my spine.

My blood seethed beneath my skin as I halted, fire coursing through me, and spun to face him. "Do you always insist on behaving like such an ass?" I shot back, struggling to keep the tremor of fury from my voice.

But he merely smirked, a wicked glint dancing in his eyes, a mocking challenge laced with something deeper— an emotion that twisted in the depths of his gaze, enticing yet elusive. "We need to rest."

"I'll be damned if I sleep out here with you." I gestured wildly toward the looming trees that seemed to close in on us like hungry shadows.

His jaw tightened like a vise, but he brushed aside my protests. "You can rest. I'll keep watch."

I let out a scoff, disbelief flooding my veins. "That's not going to happen."

He bristled at my defiance, his stormy eyes flashing with indignation. "You were willing to sleep with Eiran," he pointed out sharply.

"I was willing to do a lot of things with Eiran I'm not willing to do with you."

I watched Dacre's face twist into a mask of rage, his jaw clenched so tightly it looked like it might shatter. The darkness pooled in his eyes deepened, and tension radiated off him like heat from a volatile flame—a tempest raging just below the surface, ready to erupt at any moment.

It was clear that there was a deep-seated hatred between him and Eiran. Every time I mentioned his name, it seemed to evoke a tumultuous mix of emotions in Dacre—jealousy and anger.

My stomach twisted with guilt at the thought.

"Did you let him touch you?" His voice dripped with venom, his eyes blazing with fury. My heart raced as I faced him, my breath catching in my throat.

"How dare you ask me that question? How dare you pretend you would care?" I choked out, my throat tight with emotion.

"Of course I care," he retorted gruffly, but there was a flicker of hurt in his eyes.

"Why? You got exactly what you wanted from me. Why do you care who touches me now?" My cheeks burned with embarrassment and irritation as I spoke, my fists clenching at my sides.

"I'll never get what I want from you." His voice was harsh, which only angered me more.

"You got exactly what you wanted from me." There was so much resentment in my voice, but I couldn't hide it. "Becoming just as your father wanted you to be. Exactly like him."

"Don't say that shit again." Dacre's face contorted into a mask of fury, but I refused to back down.

"Why not?" I shot back, my words sharp and cutting. "You've always been his little soldier, haven't you?"

"Was it his idea for you to make me come before you

told me you knew who I really was?" I challenged, each word like a dagger. "Or did you come up with that all on your own?"

Our gazes locked, both of us seething with emotion.

"Trust me, Verena," he rasped out hoarsely "When I fucked you, the only person who had any part of that is me."

"Well then, don't worry." I clenched my jaw, trying to hold back the quiver in my voice. "It'll never happen again."

His laughter was stinging and cruel, twisting his lips into a mocking smirk. "Whatever you say, little traitor."

My anger flared at his words, and I wanted nothing more than to hurt him, to make him feel even a fraction of the pain he had caused me.

"The next time I come, it'll be with Eiran's name on my lips," I said boldly, trying to mask the fear in my voice.

But before I could even finish speaking, he was on me. His hands pinned me against a nearby tree, his face mere inches from mine. His eyes blazed with jealousy, and for a moment, I couldn't breathe.

"What are you doing?" I gasped, my heart racing as adrenaline coursed through my body.

"Don't ever say that shit to me again," he growled as his hand gripped the back of my neck.

My breath caught in my throat as I stared up at him. He looked like he was ready to set the world on fire, and all I could think about in that moment was how badly I wanted to burn.

"I never want to hear his name leave your lips," he seethed. "He won't touch you."

"Because you said so?" My voice trembled with both anger and uncertainty.

"Because you are mine," he declared, his words cutting through me like a knife.

I stood there speechless, taken aback by the possessiveness in his voice. But beneath it all, there was a hint of vulnerability that I had never seen before.

"Let me go," I whispered, the words catching in my throat.

He hesitated for a moment, his stormy eyes still fixed on mine before finally releasing me. We stood there in the darkness, surrounded by the heavy night air and our own unresolved feelings.

"We're stopping for the night." He left no room for argument.

I hesitated but could feel my resolve weakening under his touch, the way his fingers dug into my flesh tempting me to give in to his demands.

With a sigh, I finally relented and agreed, feeling a mixture of relief and anger. "Fine," I gritted out. "But we need to find somewhere better than this."

Dacre nodded in agreement, his gaze roaming over my body with desire. It felt like a lazy caress, igniting a fire within me.

"Let's go," he said in a low, husky voice that sent shivers down my spine. The forest loomed ahead of us, but it was his presence that unsettled me more than anything else ever could.

CHAPTER 14
DACRE

Verena's eyes had finally closed, her breathing slow and steady as she drifted into sleep. It had taken over an hour of arguing to find a suitable spot to camp for the night, and even though she stubbornly insisted that I be the one to rest, I could see the exhaustion etched in the lines of her face.

The moon hung low in the sky, casting its gentle silver glow upon us. The light filtered through the leaves and branches above, creating a mesmerizing dance of shadows on the forest floor, and as she slept, I couldn't help but watch the delicate curve of her neck illuminated by the moon's soft touch.

Despite her demands to stay as far away from me as possible, I couldn't help but yearn for her presence. It gnawed at me, this desire to have her near me, and although I knew I was unworthy of it, I couldn't help but crave the touch of her skin against mine.

My gaze swept over the dense line of trees before settling back on her. The gentle rise and fall of her chest, the soft flicker of her eyelids; she looked so at ease, and I realized that it was such a stark contrast to the restless energy that seemed to emanate from her when she was awake. But in this moment, bathed in moonlight, she appeared serene and content, like a sleeping nymph nestled among the roots of the forest.

I straightened my tired body and scanned the stillness of the surrounding forest. There were no signs of anyone following us, but I couldn't shake the sense of unease that seemed to weigh down on me like a heavy cloak.

The image of her with that soldier earlier flashed in my mind, igniting a white-hot rage within me. He had touched her, hurt her. He had breathed her in as if she belonged to him. It made me want to do more than just throw my dagger into his throat. If it hadn't been for her safety, I would have.

The mere thought of anyone laying a hand on her made me want to slaughter every soldier in the king's army. The very idea of harm coming to her filled me with a fierce desire for vengeance, and I couldn't fathom sparing those in the rebellion who would dare lay a finger on her either. The rebellion was my home, they were my people, but my rage knew no bounds when it came to her.

With cautious steps, I circled the perimeter of where she slept, scanning every possible direction for any signs of danger. Only when I was certain that we were safe did I allow myself to approach her. She lay curled up in a tight ball, her head resting against her arm. Errant strands of hair had broken free from her braid and cascaded around her face. Dirt smudges adorned her nose and chin, and she was utterly captivating.

I settled down beside her, mere inches separating us. I stretched out my legs in front of me and kept a vigilant watch over our surroundings before turning my gaze to her. Had I been this consumed with watching her every move before she left? The way she slept now had become an obsession, every rise and fall of her chest, the subtle twitches of her nose as she dreamed. It was as if I was consumed by her, every breath proving to me that she was alive. The air she breathed sustained me.

I averted my gaze and took in the forest around me, the towering trees providing a sense of seclusion and safety. My mind raced as I desperately tried to come up with a plan. I knew I had to get her to the border, to the southern coast, and onto a ship. Despite having enough coins to secure her passage twice over, I was acutely aware of the danger that awaited us on either side.

Sailors were not known for their hospitality toward runaway girls seeking passage, and they certainly wouldn't be eager to take on an heir who had fled from her cruel father, who fled from the king. But even if it meant shoving her into the cargo hold and sending her off like a piece of baggage, I would do it without hesitation.

There was no way I was going to let her return to her father or my own. The mere thought sent shivers down my spine. She would either end up dead or worse, at their mercy once again.

This unforgiving kingdom had not been kind to her, and

I prayed to the gods that the next one would be. I tried to imagine who she would become there, the life she would lead in a land untouched by her father.

Would she fall in love with a fisherman who lived in a quaint cottage on the windswept coast, his calloused hands cradling her face as if she were the most precious thing in the world to him? A man who had no inkling of the gilded cage she had left behind? Would she bear his children, their faces dotted with soft cinnamon freckles and their eyes warm like hers?

I hated the thought with a searing, visceral passion that threatened to consume me. The very idea of her finding solace in another's arms, of her laughter echoing for him to hear, of her hands cradling children that were not mine—it tore at my heart with talons of jealousy and regret.

I had never permitted myself to ponder such thoughts with anyone else, never dared to dream beyond the boundaries of my reality. But with her, everything felt different. She was going to leave this kingdom on a ship, its sails destined to catch the wind and carry her far from me, and I would stand there, rooted in place, watching her silhouette fade against the horizon.

In that moment, I let my mind wander to the possibilities of what could happen if I stepped onto that ship with her.

I reached out and delicately brushed a strand of hair away from her peaceful face. She stirred in her slumber, and I froze, my fingertips lingering against the soft skin of her cheek, just below one of those freckles I had imagined.

A gentle sigh escaped her lips as she unconsciously leaned into my touch.

She was asleep, completely unaware that it was my hand caressing her skin. And yet, my stomach was in knots as I watched her.

"Dacre," she whispered my name so softly that I questioned if I had simply imagined it. Was I so exhausted and delirious from lack of sleep that hearing my name fall from her lips was enough to drive me to the brink of madness?

"I'm here," I murmured, trailing my knuckles down her cheekbone and along the curve of her jaw.

My gaze drifted down to her lips, full and soft, and every fiber of my being yearned to wake her up and kiss her until we both lost ourselves in each other.

I wanted to take my time with her, to savor every moment, something I had foolishly neglected the first time around. I'd been so wrapped in my own anger and the betrayal of it all that I hadn't been able to see past it. But now, sitting here watching her sleep, it was hard to see anything other than her.

I was a complete idiot, and she...she was something else entirely. Too good for me, too good for this kingdom, for this world.

"I'm cold." Her voice was filled with sleep as she murmured these words without opening her eyes. Her body barely moved as she shifted closer to me.

Without hesitation, I reached out and pulled her into me. She curled up next to me, resting her head in my lap as her legs intertwined with mine, searching for warmth.

And every point where our bodies touched felt like it was burning, as if tiny sparks were igniting along my skin. I had been craving her touch, consumed by thoughts of the game Eiran was playing with her, of the way he was convincing her to trust him when he was doing nothing but betraying her.

But now, as she sought comfort in my presence, peace washed over me. Her nearness acted like a balm, soothing my restless heart and calming the tempest of emotions that had been raging within.

I leaned my head back against the rough bark of the tree, its gnarled roots digging into the ground below. My eyes traced the glittering constellations above, each one twinkling like a promise or a warning. The sky was a vast expanse of inky blackness, dotted with brilliant stars that seemed to go on forever. I couldn't help but wonder what it would look like from her perspective once she reached the next kingdom.

Will the same stars continue to shine for her once she was gone? Will they mock me with their unchanging brilliance, taunting me with the fact that she was no longer mine?

"Verena." Her name was whispered, its soft echo ringing through the dense woods. My heart pounded in my chest as I frantically scanned the area for the source, every nerve on edge with fear.

"Verena." The name reverberated through the air, urgent and growing nearer with each passing moment. My heart raced, a cold knot forming in my stomach as recognition dawned on me. It was Eiran's voice—deep and familiar, yet

laced with an unmistakable urgency that sent shivers down
my spine.

Fuck.

I gently shook Verena's shoulder, trying not to startle
her as I woke her up. Her eyes fluttered open, and her gaze
met mine, hazy and unfocused from slumber.

With a sense of urgency, I whispered, "Get up. Someone's here."

Fear immediately flashed across her face like a bolt of
lightning in the darkness.

She glanced down at the spot where she had been sleeping, tangled up with me, and with a jolt of realization,
scrambled away to her feet.

The cool air bit at my skin where she had just been as I
followed suit, instinctively unsheathing my dagger, its
blade glinting in the soft moonlight.

"Verena. It's Eiran," Eiran's voice called out again.

I caught Verena's startled expression—a mixture of
surprise and uncertainty—and felt a surge of anxiety wash
over me. Would she choose him over me?

"We need to hide," I said, my voice low and urgent as I
grasped her hand in mine. Her fingers were soft and pliable,
neither resisting nor reciprocating my touch.

"Verena," he called out once more, this time sounding
dangerously close.

"Verena, we need to hide now," I repeated, my heart
pounding in my chest.

My frustration grew at the thought of cowering from
him, the bitter taste of fear and anger mixing in my mouth.
But above all else, I needed to keep Verena safe.

But she hesitated, her eyes wide with uncertainty, and when he called out her name again, it was only a few feet away, the crunch of leaves under his heavy footsteps growing louder.

"Fuck," I cursed under my breath, the word hissing through clenched teeth as I pulled her behind me. "You need to run. Head south as quickly as you can. Do not stop for anyone. Do not come back, no matter what you hear."

I pulled the coins from my pocket and thrust them into her palm. She glanced down at them, confusion etched on her face until I closed her hand around them firmly.

"That should buy you passage onto any ship," I said through gritted teeth, desperately trying to keep my emotions in check. I didn't have time to consider the worst, to think about the possibility that I could never see her again. "You do not stop until you get to the docks. Find the first captain you see and offer it all."

I stole a quick glance behind me, making sure we were still alone before turning back to her. "I will try to meet you there, but do not wait for me."

She didn't respond, but I could see fear and determination etched into every line of her face. Letting go of her hand, I slipped into the shadows.

"Dacre," she whispered my name and the desperation in that one word was enough to break me.

"Run, Verena." I disappeared from sight before I did something foolish, something that my heart ached for but would not protect her the way I needed to.

Instead, I moved through the forest as quickly as I

could, leaving her behind until Eiran finally came into view.

I stepped out of the shadow of trees, and his eyes widened in surprise at the sight of me. "Looking for someone?" I pushed my hands into my pockets, nonchalantly leaning against a tree as I took him in.

"Dacre." He let out a sharp exhale, his tone laced with disbelief and a tinge of bitterness. He had no idea that Verena was with me. He didn't know that I was the one who had killed a soldier to save her, the one who had taken her away from him.

I took in his appearance, noticing the wildness in his gaze and the disheveled state of his clothes. They were tattered and stained with dirt, but he didn't appear to be injured. His eyes locked onto mine, filled with a sense of desperation.

"I'm looking for Verena," he stated, his voice wavering slightly.

"As is the rest of the kingdom," I replied casually. "Any luck?"

"Don't be an asshole," he retorted sharply. "Is she with you?"

My mind raced as I debated on what to tell him, and after a moment of hesitation, I answered honestly, "No, she's not with me. Have you seen her?"

Eiran paused, his expression pained as if considering whether or not he should tell me the truth, and to my surprise, he did. "She was with me for a few days. We were ambushed by the king's men...I don't know if they took her."

There was a trembling panic in his voice that surprised me. Was he truly fearful for what might happen to Verena or was he scared of my father's wrath once he realized that he hadn't been able to keep his hold on her?

"Yet you're still headed south instead of north where they would have taken her," I remarked, my voice laced with frustration, the words sharp and biting.

Eiran let his face fall into a mask of indifference, but a flicker of uncertainty danced in his eyes. "Like I said, I don't know if they took her or if she managed to run. Our plan was for her to run."

"You and her are making plans now?" I asked, my voice dripping with sarcasm. I crossed one ankle over the other, the leather of my boots creaking softly as I shifted. There was still pain in my thigh that lingered from her dagger. I hadn't been able to heal myself fully, not after using so much of my magic to heal her battered body. Magic came at a cost, and I was paying for it now.

With deliberate slowness, I pulled my dagger from its worn leather sheath, the metal gleaming dully in the dim light. I ran the razor-sharp blade beneath my nail, methodically scraping out the accumulated grime and dirt. The soft scraping sound filled the tense silence between us, a subtle yet unmistakable threat lingering in the air.

"I'm doing what you should have done. I'm taking care of our people," he growled, his voice lowered and filled with a simmering anger.

"And how exactly does Verena fit into that?" I narrowed my eyes, challenging him.

"If you had listened to your father and brought her to

him when he asked, instead of doing only the gods know what, we wouldn't be in this mess," he scolded me, his eyes flashing with accusation.

"You mean fucking her." I couldn't help but glance up at him, my heart racing as I saw the anger take over his face. A storm was brewing in his eyes, and I knew I was pushing him too far. Verena would be furious when she found out what I had said, but in that moment, I didn't care. "What Verena and I were doing while my father wanted to use her as a pawn was fucking." I leaned forward, meeting his furious gaze. "I fucked her until she called out my name in the softest little whimper."

"I know the exact sound you're talking about." Eiran's grin made him look almost deranged as he tilted his head slightly, watching me closely. "But it wasn't your name on her lips when I heard it."

"You fucking…" I charged toward him, but I froze in my tracks as a booming voice echoed through the air.

"Boys." The crunching of leaves and twigs beneath heavy boots pierced the quiet forest air, announcing my father's arrival. Emerging from between the trees, he was flanked by Reed and Adler. My muscles tensed and my jaw clenched as I watched them approach. "I think that's more than enough, don't you?" he said, voice dripping with authority.

My father stood imposingly before me. His face was stern and commanding, his eyes piercing and unyielding. But I didn't back down, standing tall and meeting his gaze head-on.

"Son, it's nice to see you again," he said with false warmth. "We thought you had gotten lost."

"No," I shook my head defiantly. "I'm doing exactly what you wanted me to do. I'm trying to find the heir."

My father's eyes flickered with annoyance before settling on Eiran, who stood nearby. "That was what he was doing," my father said, pointing a finger at Eiran. "He had the heir in his grasp and was supposed to meet us at the southern border with her, but somehow that got messed up."

My father studied me carefully, too carefully. I knew he could see right through my facade.

"Eiran had told me that he couldn't hold off the king's men long enough to escape with the heir," I said casually, my voice betraying none of the rage boiling inside me, even though every fiber of my being yearned to slam my fist into Eiran's smug jaw. The urge for violence pulsed through my veins, barely contained beneath a thin veneer of civility. He had meticulously cultivated her trust, weaving an intricate web of lies and false promises, and even though I was already painfully aware of his treachery, this stark reminder ignited a murderous fury within me.

"It's odd, isn't it?" My father cocked his head, watching me carefully. "Eiran was able to kill every soldier he came across, yet he couldn't keep one girl in his grasp."

"Do you think she went willingly?" I asked, my voice trembling slightly as I tried to sound convincing.

"With someone, yes," my father replied coolly. "I'm just not certain it was one of the king's men."

With each measured step he took toward me, his eyes

grew colder and sharper. The knot in my stomach tightened painfully, twisting like a coiled serpent as I could feel the unspoken accusations burning through me like white-hot brands. My palms began to sweat, growing clammy and slick, while my heart raced wildly in my chest, pounding against my rib cage as if begging me to flee.

Fuck.

"Do you have her, Dacre?" my father demanded, his voice a low rumble that sent shivers down my spine. The weight of my father's gaze bore down on me like a heavy cloak, each word he spoke rumbling through my bones. His eyes were like shards of ice, cold and calculating, as they assessed my every move.

I tried to maintain a composed facade, but my hands betrayed me with their trembling. "I already told Eiran that I didn't."

But my father's eyes only narrowed further, suspicion etched into every line of his face. "Then why did you leave camp in the middle of the night?"

"I'm looking for the heir." I crossed my arms over my chest as I watched my father, preparing myself for a fight if that was what it came to.

"You told me she ran back in Enveilorian, but it seems that's not the whole truth, is it?" He paused, studying me closely. I could see the wheels turning in his mind as he tried to decipher my every move, trying to see if I was hiding something from him. "You claimed she ran, but you decided to leave the camp by yourself because you were certain the girl would seek you out if you were alone."

"I didn't…" I shook my head, but my father cut me off.

"Did she share any of her secrets with you while you were forgetting about your loyalties, buried inside her?" His voice was cold and sharp.

"I don't know any of her secrets," I answered honestly. "She had no reason to trust me with them."

He didn't believe me. It was written all over his face as he watched me, and his sharp gaze shifted toward Eiran as he commanded, "Find her."

Eiran took a step forward as if he was going to pass me, but I planted myself firmly in his path.

"That's not going to work for me." My words came out as a low growl, my anger simmering just below the surface.

My father's gaze met mine, sparks of fury igniting in his eyes. "I'm sorry?"

"I won't allow you to hurt her."

"Do you think I care about what you will allow? This is about the kingdom, boy. And you have put us in a position of weakness by losing her in the first place." His voice dripped with disdain. "Get out of the way."

My father's eyes narrowed into slits, but I couldn't bring myself to step aside.

"I overheard you and Reed." I nodded to the man behind him, to Eiran's father. "Do you really believe that the king will be lured out because of her? Do you truly think he will give up the reserves when he's bled this kingdom dry building it?"

"What I believe is that his heir had no business being inside our rebellion to start with, but it was you who brought her there." His expression hardened, his pupils flaring. "Why was she there, Dacre?"

"I found her beneath the palace. Thrown into the dungeons just as your daughter was." I let my mind go back to that day. She had looked so small, so broken.

But she had never been fragile.

"I was taught to protect our people, remember? And she had the rebellion mark upon her skin."

"That's odd, isn't it?" He crossed his arms, and I could practically see the wheels turning as he searched my eyes. "Why would the heir to the king be in those dungeons? Why would she possess our mark?"

My chest ached with the weight of my words, as if I were betraying Verena with every syllable. But she was not our enemy; she was not her father. "Have you ever considered that Verena isn't the traitor that you think she is?"

His response was sharp and filled with anger. "What I think is that my son is a fool."

"You're not going to hurt her."

My father scoffed, dismissive of my words. "What I will and won't do with the heir is none of your business."

"You want me to be the future king if you overtake this kingdom, but it's not my business what you do with her?" I shook my head and cast a sideways glance at Eiran. He stood rooted to the spot, his body tense and alert, like a statue waiting with bated breath for my father's commands.

My father's face contorted with rage, his features hardening into a mask of fury. He stalked toward me, each footfall echoing through the dense forest around us. "You'll be fortunate if you make it through this with your life," he snarled. "Do not dare to disobey my orders, lest you face the full weight of its consequences."

"I won't help you find her." My heart pounded in my chest, each beat a reminder of the grave consequences that lay ahead. It seemed as though the world had slowed, each drop of perspiration rolling down my brow a testament to the anxiety that snaked its tendrils around my very being.

But I was prepared to accept whatever consequences awaited me as long as she got away.

"Then you leave me no choice," my father growled, his voice edged with danger. "Seize him."

His men moved toward me. Eiran did as well, and I prepared myself for their attack. If my father thought they were going to take me willingly, he was wrong.

My heart beat wildly, adrenaline surging through my veins as I prepared to fight.

They stood before me, these men who were meant to be my people, and they were prepared to take me as their prisoner.

I was his son, yet he cared more that I hadn't given him the king's daughter.

I stood my ground, my eyes locked with my father's, and clenched my fists.

"You're a coward, Father." My voice trembling with emotion. "You're willing to sacrifice everything, including your own son, to maintain your power. You're no better than the king you despise."

My father's face twisted in anger, and he moved to strike me, but one of his men held him back. Eiran took advantage of my distraction and charged at me, his shoulder slamming into my stomach and knocking the breath from my lungs.

As I hit the ground, gasping for air, Eiran landed on top of me. He didn't dare give me a chance to catch my breath. Instead, he threw a punch, managing to connect with my jaw.

It echoed through the stillness of the forest, and a flare of pain raced across my face. With a grunt, I rolled to the side, attempting to break free from his grasp.

"You're a fool," Eiran said close to my face. "You're throwing away everything we've worked for, for a girl."

I barely allowed him to get the last word past his lips before I threw my elbow up, landing it against his temple.

He stumbled sideways, rubbing his head, and I saw my chance. I bucked him off me completely and climbed to my feet as quickly as I could.

Eiran still looked dazed from my hit, but his father wasn't. He hit me with a blow that took me by surprise, and Adler caught one of my hands in his before I could defend myself.

I thrashed and writhed, my body fighting against his iron grip. The force of the hit sent my head spinning and blurred my vision. As I gasped for air, I could hear the rhythmic rise and fall of our breaths, a symphony of struggle in the otherwise serene forest.

Every muscle in my body tensed as I braced for another strike, but it was my father's words that hit me next. "You have disappointed me, Dacre."

I met his gaze, my own eyes filled with defiance.

Eiran's father managed to seize my other arm, his

fingers digging into my flesh. I fought against their combined strength, my muscles straining futilely.

With a brutal force, they shoved me backward, pinning me against a gnarled tree.

The rough bark scraped against my back as they slammed me into the unyielding wood, knocking the wind from my lungs.

My father's face suddenly loomed before me, his eyes dark with rage, nostrils flaring. For a split second, I saw the veins bulging in his neck and the tendons standing out in his forearm. Then his fist crashed into my stomach like a battering ram, driving deep into my abdomen. Pain exploded through my core as the air whooshed out of me in a strangled gasp.

I doubled over and struggled to catch my breath. My vision blurred as tears stung at the corners of my eyes. I could feel Reed's hands on my shoulders as he pulled me back upright until I faced my father once again.

"You think you can defy me, boy?" my father snarled. "You forget your place."

I didn't answer him. Maybe he was right, maybe I had forgotten my place, but I couldn't bring myself to regret it.

His fist rammed into my stomach again, the impact jolting me with a force that was somehow harder than the last. I dug deep within myself, searching for any reserve of power or strength, but only found exhaustion.

With each blow, my body convulsed and trembled with pain. The force of his fist against my skin like a physical manifestation of the greed that had been consuming him.

"Take him away." My father's voice thundered, shattering the tense silence.

Their grips tightened on my arms, sending sharp bolts of pain shooting through me as they began to forcefully pull me forward.

A shock wave of power pulsed from my core, vibrating the very air around me. My power. No. *Her* power.

My father's expression shifted from smug triumph to stunned surprise as a force slammed into his chest. He stumbled backward, his body crashing to the ground.

As Eiran's eyes widened in disbelief, Verena emerged from the shadows of the trees, her form bathed in the moonlight filtering through the leaves. Tension etched her features, her jaw clenched as if she were holding back a torrent of power.

"Let him go," she commanded, the sound of her voice sending a chill down my spine, making me shiver involuntarily.

"Well, well, if it isn't the princess," my father sneered as he wiped blood from his split lip with the back of his hand. "And yet, my son was just so adamant that he hadn't seen you."

Verena's piercing gaze never faltered; her eyes locked onto his with an intensity that could set the world ablaze. Her anger was palpable, radiating from her in waves that threatened to engulf everything and everyone around her.

"It would appear that he might be taking after his father." She held her hands out at her sides, fingers splayed and ready to unleash her magic. The air hummed with energy, charged by the sheer force of her fury. "You are nothing but a liar, after all."

My father grinned smugly, his eyes darting between Verena and me as if enjoying the chaos he had caused. "It appears that you take after your parents as well. I met your mother a few times. She was such a good whore for the king. It's good to see you're holding up the family tradition."

Verena's eyes blazed with a fierce fury, and a bolt of raw energy surged through me like wildfire. It seared through my veins, igniting every nerve in my body and setting my senses alight. Both men let out agonized yells as the force seemed to burn them, their hands recoiling from me as if I were a scorching flame. My gaze flicked between them and I saw Reed stare down at his trembling hands, shock and fear etched into his features as he stumbled backward.

My father was climbing to his feet, his hand clutching his chest as if trying to contain the inferno raging within him.

But it was too late. The power within me surged, a tempest of raw energy begging to be unleashed. I felt Verena's presence beside me, her own magic humming and crackling in harmony with mine.

What was that?

"You are no better than my father." She was still staring directly at mine, her eyes ablaze with a fury that rivaled the sun itself. "You want to abolish a king, only to replace him with one just as ruthless." Her voice carried a weight that seemed to shake the very ground beneath our feet.

My father laughed, the sound cold and angry. "Yet you were hiding away from him in my city." My father pointed at his chest. "You sought refuge from us, but now you damn us?" My father glared at her, and me at her side, with hatred burning in his eyes. "You damn my son?"

Verena's eyes narrowed, gleaming with a fierce intensity as she stepped forward, her magic swirling around her like the chaotic winds. Dark tendrils of energy danced in the air, shimmering with an unsettling beauty.

My feet instinctively followed hers, each step echoing the tumultuous rhythm of her resolve as I moved in line just behind her. As my fingertips gently brushed against her back—a soft, unspoken gesture of solidarity—I felt the tension radiate from her. She straightened, exuding an air of defiance that made her seem larger than life.

"What will you do with me?" she demanded, her voice reverberating among the trees. "You sent Eiran after me, you sent him to betray my trust. There's no telling how many men you sent into this dark wood, and for what?"

Eiran's eyes darted away, his jaw clenching at her words.

"For the good of the kingdom," my father sneered, his voice echoing dangerously in the stillness. "You will be used for the good of the kingdom."

"She won't be used at all." I couldn't stop the words from falling past my lips.

"And who do you think will stop me?" My father's gaze met mine, a mirror of who I was to become. His words hung in the air, heavy with accusation and poison.

Verena's hands lifted with an air of defiance, as if she

was going to prove exactly who it was that would stop them. I could feel her power emanating from within me, intertwined with my own. It surged through my veins, filling me with strength that I lacked on my own.

My arms reached out instinctively, mirroring her movements. I let the power unleash from my fingertips, her black smoke pouring out of me in a way that magic never had before, and it slammed into the four of them, sending them flying backward.

Adler's back slammed into one of the nearby trees with an earth-shattering thud. His body lay sprawled on the ground, his once powerful limbs now limp and lifeless. His eyes now dull and hollow.

I had killed him.

I locked eyes with my father as I wrapped Verena's hand in my own. If he had thought me a traitor before, then I was much worse now.

I was their enemy.

The son of the rebellion, yet I was choosing her.

I had killed one of them for her.

"We need to go," I whispered urgently to her, my hand gripping hers as we turned. She nodded once, her hand squeezing mine tightly as we took off before any of them could get to their feet.

CHAPTER 15
VERENA

We didn't stop until the sun rose and fell again, the night sky now giving way to the fiery hues of orange and pink across the sky as the sun rose yet again.

The rhythmic sound of waves filled the air, their salty scent immediately evocative of memories and places I had longed to forget.

Since I was just a child, my eyes had been drawn to the horizon outside my window, yearning for the boundless expanse of the Northern Sea. But as we emerged from the cover of the forest and the Southern Sea came into view, conflicting emotions washed over me. The endless blue waters, once a symbol of hope, now seemed to mock me with its impossible promises.

The vast expanse of the ocean stretched out before me, its waves crashing against the rocky shoreline with an untamed force. The sea seemed to merge seamlessly with the small coastal town, as if it were a living being that breathed in and out with the tide.

"We need to be quick." Dacre broke the silence between us, his eyes searching the woods that we had just left. He was tired, his body moving slower than I had ever seen before. "My father won't be far behind."

His father who he had betrayed. The father who he turned his back on for me.

He had *killed* one of them for me.

Our words had dried up, lost in the urgency of our escape. We ran as fast as our legs could carry us, our feet pounding against the unforgiving ground while our lungs strained for air. The only sounds were our hurried breaths and the thudding rhythm of our footsteps, a desperate beat propelling us forward.

But even as we fled, my mind was in chaos. Thoughts swirled like a whirlwind, each one demanding answers I couldn't give. The remnants of my power still lingered in my veins, *our power.* I couldn't understand it, couldn't wrap my head around the sheer force that had coursed through me.

But I knew that it saved us.

He had saved me.

He saved me, healed me, then gave up everything he knew.

I felt foolish to trust him, naive to let my guard down with anyone, yet every time I looked at him, my doubts slipped further from my grip.

My heart pounded wildly in my chest as I nodded, following Dacre down the gentle slope of the hill.

The coastal town sprawled out before me, larger and more vibrant than I had ever imagined. The streets were alive with a constant flow of people, each one absorbed in their own tasks and errands.

The salty tang of the sea mingled with the mouth-watering scent of freshly caught seafood, creating an intoxicating blend that filled the air.

Our footsteps echoed against the cobblestone streets as we passed by a colorful cart overflowing with an array of freshly baked pastries. The sweet, buttery scent drifted toward us, making my stomach churn in hunger.

Beside it, a cart displayed an assortment of vibrant spices, their fragrant aromas dancing in the air. Despite its similarities to the capital city, this bustling marketplace was full of unique sights and smells.

As we weaved through the crowd, I couldn't help but marvel at this world beyond what I knew.

It was an unknown corner of my own kingdom, hidden behind the veil of familiarity and routine, and I couldn't help but wonder what other secrets and wonders lay just beyond my reach.

When I had imagined the southern coast, my mind had conjured up images of quaint cottages and a charming village nestled by the sea.

But what I saw around us was far from that expectation. It was a bustling town filled with homes and shops and winding streets.

This was something my father never told me about.

Dacre's firm grip enveloped my hand, his calloused fingers intertwining with mine as he pulled me along behind him. His steely gaze remained fixed ahead, determined and unwavering, as if he feared losing sight of our destination for even a moment.

Every muscle in his body seemed taut and ready for action, his steps purposeful and swift as we made our way forward. I could feel the weight of his focused energy radiating from him, urging us on with each step we took.

"We must reach the docks," Dacre insisted, his firm grasp pulling me closer to his side. I could feel the heat of his body and allowed myself to be drawn in by his warmth and strength.

He was right.

The docks were my only hope, the gateway to a new life and a chance at freedom. Anxiety coiled in my veins as we hurried toward the teeming harbor, our fate hanging on the success of boarding one of those ships.

I had nothing but the cold metal of the coins that Dacre had thrust into my hand, no connections to offer, and no valid reason for any captain to allow me passage aboard their ship.

But I prayed to the gods that one of them did.

Dacre's strong arms pulled me closer, enveloping me in a protective embrace as we turned sharply to the right. My heart raced as I strained to catch a glimpse of what lay ahead, but Dacre shielded me from view with his broad frame.

Through a small opening between his arms, I caught sight of three heavily armed King's Guards marching down the street toward us.

Dacre quickened our pace as we darted down a narrow

side street, the pungent smell of ale wafting through the air.

The street was crowded with people, mostly sailors and merchants, their voices echoing off the stone walls. But they paid us no mind as we hurried past them.

Dacre's fingers tensed around mine as he led us toward a quaint inn at the end of the street. The scent of ale grew more potent as we strolled past a tavern, where raucous laughter could be heard spilling out onto the cobblestone road.

Dacre pushed open the door to the inn, the wooden frame creaking loudly. The inside was dark and cramped, filled with trinkets and books.

Without a word, Dacre guided me to a small desk tucked in the corner of the room. The door behind us slammed shut with a resounding thud, trapping us inside.

The stagnant heat in the room was stifling. The stillness in the room only broken by the small fan held by the older woman seated behind the desk.

The woman's wrinkled hand clutched onto the fan as if it were a lifeline, her weary eyes reflecting the exhaustion of the long day even though the sun had just risen. Beads of sweat glistened on her forehead as her gaze flicked back and forth between Dacre and me.

"Do you have any vacancies?" Dacre asked and pressed a hand against the wooden desk.

The innkeeper nodded, reaching for a key with delicate fingers. She reached deep into a drawer, her hand disappearing for a few moments before emerging with the key. "One."

"We'll take it."

Dacre reached into my pocket and pulled out five gleaming coins and tossed them onto the desk, causing the innkeeper's eyes to light up with excitement. She eagerly took the currency, her hand shaking slightly as she counted it out. "I'll just need to change the bedding. It's been vacant for some time."

"We don't mind," Dacre replied urgently, his voice betraying a sense of panic. "We need the room now, and I'll give you three more of those coins if we can have food brought up as well."

The innkeeper readily agreed, nodding and handing over the key to our room. "Up the stairs, first room on the right."

"Thank you."

The woman's eyes locked onto mine, her gaze searching. I shifted uncomfortably, my body instinctively wanting to shrink away from her knowing stare. My hair fell like a curtain over my face, shielding me from her perceptive eyes as we turned away from her.

As we made our way up the narrow stairs to our room, I couldn't shake off the feeling of unease that lingered in the pit of my stomach. The woman's piercing gaze seemed to have seen through me, and I couldn't help but wonder if she knew who I was.

If she knew who the king's men were looking for.

With a creak, Dacre slid in the key before opening the door to our room, revealing a small but tidy space. The dim light from a lone window cast shadows across the walls, highlighting the worn and faded wallpaper.

In the center of the room sat a single bed, its sheets wrinkled and thin. I crossed my arms, feeling the weight of uncertainty settle in my stomach as Dacre shut the door behind us.

"We need to get to the ships," I urged.

"I need to get to the ships. You are gonna stay here," Dacre replied, his tone firm as he ran his fingers through his hair. But I could see the fear in his eyes, betraying his confident words.

He was panicked.

This wasn't a part of the plan. My mind raced with questions and doubts, unsure of what to do next.

"You must remain here, hidden and safe. Eat when food is brought to you, but do not open the door for anyone else." His fingers traced over the door absentmindedly as he spoke. "I will try to secure your passage on a ship and return as soon as possible." He tucked the key into his pocket. "Remember, do not let anyone in this door. There are far too many people after you here."

"I want to come with you," I pleaded, my voice betraying the hesitation and fear in my mind.

Dacre was leaving me here alone, and I could sense the same fear and panic radiating from him. But amid it all, there was still a trace of lingering doubt—what if this was all just another betrayal?

"Listen to me, Verena." Dacre's hands were warm and firm as they gripped my shoulders. His voice was urgent and laced with fear. "If those king's men find us, find you, they're going to take you. And I won't be able to fight them off alone. I have no power in this town. My father won't be far behind." He shook his head, his eyes full of worry. "I need you to stay hidden until we can get you on a ship. It's our only option, your only choice."

The weight of his words settled heavily on my chest.

Trusting him was my only choice.

That was what he meant.

That's what he wouldn't say out loud, but it was the truth.

Either I trusted him, or I was on my own.

"Fine." I crossed my arms and looked up at him. "But if you aren't back in two hours, I'm leaving this inn."

Dacre's eyes locked onto mine, a mixture of relief and desperation in his glance. He nodded. "Two hours," he murmured before he stepped back from me. "If I'm not back, leave, Verena. Find another way. Trust your instincts, but don't let them capture you. Promise me that."

I nodded, knowing that I didn't have much of a choice. "I promise."

Dacre's face relaxed slightly as if he had just released a heavy burden from his shoulders. He leaned in and pressed his lips gently against my cheek.

I leaned into his touch, allowing myself to revel in the feel of him before he turned and left the room, the door creaking closed behind him.

I quickly turned the lock, hearing the latch echo through the room like an omen.

I was alone in that small room, with nothing but the constant sound of the sea on the horizon. A sense of dread filled my chest, but I knew I had no other choice but to wait.

CHAPTER 16
DACRE

With a quick, anxious glance over my shoulder, I bounded up the stairs, my arms overflowing with an assortment of items. My heart raced as I fumbled in my pocket for the key, the weight of it cool and steady against my fingers.

I pressed my ear to the door, listening for any sounds as I grasped the cool metal of the key. I couldn't hear anything, and I wondered if Verena was sleeping.

I took a deep breath and inserted the key into the lock, turning it slowly. The door swung open silently, revealing the dimly lit room inside. I stepped in cautiously, closing the door behind me with a soft click.

Verena was nowhere to be found, but the room was thick with a hot, sticky steam that enveloped me like a dense fog. I strained my ears and could just barely make out her soft humming coming from the bathroom, weaving its way through the steam like a melody.

I let out a sigh of relief and made my way over to the bed, setting down the items in my arms. I sank down onto the bed gratefully, the worn fabric softening the ache in my muscles, the ache that still plagued my damn thigh. My eyes were heavy with fatigue as I let the exhaustion seep into my bones.

My father had been prepared to take me back as a prisoner. I was his son, the person he claimed to have trusted most in the world once upon a time, and I had obliterated that trust.

I had killed one of his most trusted men.

For her.

My gaze drifted toward the bathroom, where the door stood slightly ajar. Thin wisps of steam escaped into the room, carrying subtle hints of lavender.

She was still humming, the tune foreign to my ears, but somehow comforting.

From my seat, I could just make out the fogged-up mirror through the door. Despite its haziness, it was impossible to miss her form as she rose from the steaming bath and reached for a towel.

My eyes should have respectfully averted, giving her the privacy she deserved, but I couldn't tear my gaze away.

The moisture from the hot water glistened on her smooth skin, highlighting every curve and contour of her body. Her hair cascaded down her back in dark, wet strands, like a siren beckoning me closer.

Every inch of her was like an intoxicating drug, and I was hopelessly addicted. No matter how much I tried to resist, I couldn't stop myself from devouring every detail I could make out in that tantalizing moment.

She pressed the towel against her chest, soaking up the water there before her eyes met mine in the mirror.

A sudden urge of warmth spread through my body, and my heart thundered in my chest.

My eyes were helplessly drawn to her, and I couldn't look away. But to my surprise, she didn't shy away from my gaze either. Instead, she met my stare head-on, her eyes burning with an intensity that held me captive.

She moved the towel over her body in agonizingly slow motions. My eyes followed the gentle glide of the fabric against her skin, almost as if I were in a trance.

She bent forward, her eyes never leaving mine once, her body glistening with droplets of water as she held the top of the towel against her chest and ran the other end along her legs. The dim light from the bathroom cast shadows on her curves, highlighting every slope and dip of her figure.

My hands clenched tightly at my sides, fighting the urge to invade her space and claim what I had no right to.

My eyes raked over her body, tracing every inch with hungry eyes. My heart clenched at the thought of any injuries marring her body. I longed to run my hands over her skin, to feel its smoothness and search for any signs of harm.

And gods, I wanted to taste her.

My breath hitched as I struggled to maintain my composure. Her stormy gaze held mine, unflinching, as she expertly wrapped the towel around her body, every move calculated and torturous.

As she emerged from the steam-filled bathroom, droplets of water still clung to her skin like jewels. Her hair cascaded in wet waves down her back, and time seemed to slow as I traced my eyes down the subtle arch of her waist.

The air was thick with unspoken apologies and unfulfilled desires. My hands trembled at my sides, aching to reach out and beg for forgiveness, to plead with her.

But I knew she had every reason not to trust me, not to trust anyone. So we stared at one another, our emotions swirling like a tempestuous storm around us, waiting for one of us to break the heavy silence that hung between us.

She hesitated, her eyes filled with doubt as she closed the distance between us. She looked away from me, her gaze falling to my side. "What's all that?" She gestured toward the items I had brought with me.

"For you," I said, my voice catching in my throat as I shifted uncomfortably and adjusted myself in my pants. "I thought you might appreciate a change of clothes. And those rebellion leathers kind of give you away this far south."

Her gaze fell back to me, to my own worn leathers. "And yours won't give you away?"

"I've got things for me as well." I swallowed, worried about how she would handle the next words that fell from my lips. "These leathers would be brutal on the ship."

Her spine stiffened, her entire body tense as she clutched her towel tightly in her hand. "You're coming with me?"

I had struggled to convince the captain to take on just one passenger, let alone two.

I had offered him all the coins I had, and he had accepted half. But it was my mother's dagger that hung at my side that he really wanted.

So, with the last thing I had left of my mother, I secured passage for us both.

"Did you really think I'd put you on a ship alone and watch you sail away from me?" I questioned, instantly regretting my admission.

She bit her lip, her eyes flickering back to the things at my side. "But your people are here. Your rebellion is here," she said, her voice cracking with emotion.

"And yet, you won't be." A sharp pain twisted in my chest, reminding me of the sacrifice that lay ahead for both of us.

She let out a deep, shuddering sigh, her lips trembling as she took a small step back. It felt like an endless expanse, a mile filled with distrust. "When do we leave?" Her voice quivered with both fear and anticipation.

"Two days." I forced out the words, my own distaste for them evident in my tone. It was the quickest I could arrange our escape from the kingdom, but it meant that for two days' time, we would be vulnerable and in danger.

"We're here for two days?" The fear in her eyes mirrored the same gnawing sensation in my gut.

"It's the quickest I could get us out of here," I said quietly.

She nodded, her eyes full of questions. "There's food for you left on the desk."

"Thank you." I nodded and dug my fingers into the thin blanket beneath me. "I think I'm going to bathe first, wash away the days of travel." *And try to drown out the wicked thoughts of you.*

I let my gaze trail down her body, down her bare thighs. Heat surged through me, a fiery desire that threatened to consume me.

She was right in front of me, so close that I could reach out and touch her, but I couldn't.

I wanted to grab her wrist and pull her closer, to beg her forgiveness with my tongue against her skin.

Everything about what we were doing was a risk. Leaving this kingdom, praying to the gods that the one we traveled to would be better, praying that her father nor mine would catch us before the sea took us away.

She was a risk.

One that I shouldn't have been willing to take, but trying to fight it was futile.

My want for her was obsessive, incessant. *Maddening.*

She had betrayed me, lied to me, and yet, I couldn't sit there and look at those wounds forever when looking up at her made me want to hide them beneath a bandage as if they never existed at all.

The wounds we caused one another were raw and pulsing, aching with the pain of our betrayals, but as I sat in front of her, I was consumed by both peace and fire.

I sprang up from the bed as if it were aflame, my heart pounding in my chest. Verena's sharp blue eyes locked onto mine, her expression a mix of surprise and something more.

The room seemed to shrink around us as the tension between us rose, crackling like fire in the air.

"Excuse me." I took a step forward, a step toward her, but she didn't move.

She was blocking my path to the bathroom, caging me in until I had nowhere to look but at her.

Our bodies were so close, I could feel the heat radiating from her skin. Every fiber in my being yearned to reach out and pull her closer. My throat felt as though it were on fire, burning with the desire to share every racing thought that plagued my mind.

But as she looked up at me, her eyes wide and vulnerable, her bottom lip trembling slightly, I couldn't find the words to express the storm inside me.

"Please." She broke the silence with a quiet exhale and took the smallest step to the side, creating just enough room for me to squeeze past her. The air felt thick and heavy, like molasses, as I carefully maneuvered around her, our bodies brushing with the lightest touch.

"Dacre." My name was a gentle plea, a whisper I could hardly hear over my raging heartbeat.

I hesitated, feeling the warmth of her body barely brushing against mine. Her gaze flickered down to my lips, her knuckles turning white from the force of her grip on her towel.

Her breath hitched, and there was so much longing on her face. It was easy to see her desire, but it was also impossible to miss her fear.

"Thank you." She nodded toward the bed. "For that, and for helping me."

Her chest heaved, her breasts rising and falling against my chest, and I leaned in, unable to resist any longer. "Don't thank me." I shook my head. "I don't deserve your thanks."

Verena's expression softened as she gazed back at me. "You may not deserve it, but it's yours."

I swallowed hard, trying not to read too much into her words.

She was mine.

"I'm so sorry, Verena." I reached out for her, but she took a small step back as if startled by my words.

"We don't need to do this." She shook her head.

"Yes. We do," I insisted, my voice low and pleading. "I was so angry, so hurt, and I should have never…"

"Bathe." She cut me off and nodded toward the bathroom, and I could see the rapid fluttering of her pulse in her neck. "We both need sleep."

I clenched my jaw and bit my tongue as I slipped past her, the subtle brush of our bodies feeling like a brand as I made my way toward the small bathroom.

My hands trembled with the urge to reach out for her, to make her look up at me as I told her the things I needed to, pleaded with her for her forgiveness.

I gently closed the door behind me with those same trembling hands, leaving me alone in the cramped room. The air was thick with the smell of lavender, and a small candle flickered by the sink, casting shadows that danced across the walls.

I undressed quickly, forcing myself not to run straight back to the room.

The worn tiles under my feet were cool against my tired skin as I turned on the knob and allowed the water to cascade over me. I leaned forward, my forearm resting on the wall as I leaned into it and tried to relax.

I clamped my eyes closed, but all I could see was her.

She was right outside that door wrapped in a towel, and I let myself picture what she was doing, what she was thinking.

I let myself imagine that she were with me. I imagined my fingers tracing the curve of her waist, the water cascading down her body, her skin soft and warm to the touch.

I dreamed that she didn't push me away, that there was no sign of doubt in her eyes when she looked up at me.

Slowly, the water began to soothe my aching muscles, and I could almost feel the warmth of her skin against mine, the softness of her hair brushing against my face, and the scent of her lingering in the air.

My thoughts raced, and I imagined every angle of her body. My fingers traced lines on my skin, longing to feel her touch, to have her wrap those fingers around me.

My fingers pressed firmly into the cool, smooth tiles of the wall, desperately seeking grounding as my mind wandered to her touch. With my other hand, I traced the curve of my hip, wishing it was her hand instead. The water cascaded down my body in a comforting rhythm, its soothing touch only increasing my longing.

As I stood there, the desire for her grew stronger, and I found myself reaching for my own body, needing to feel her touch, though it was only an illusion. I wrapped my hand around myself, and I was so hard.

My imagination ran wild with thoughts of her touch, her lips, her skin, and I pumped my cock in my hand as my breathing became heavier.

I remembered the small sounds she made when I touched her, when I tasted her. I was haunted by the memory of her whimper when she called out my name as if I were the only thing in the world she had ever wanted.

My thoughts were consumed by her, and I yearned for her touch. I needed to feel her, to be close to her, to be inside her. I could practically feel the tightness of her walls, the wetness of her desire, and the intensity of her passion as I thrust into her.

There was a sound just outside the door, pulling me from my fantasy, but I didn't stop as I turned my head to look. I could see the shadows of her feet where she stood near the door, and I allowed myself to imagine that she leaned back against it as she listened to me try to get myself off with thoughts of her.

I groaned as I squeezed myself harder. The water splashed down my face, trailing over my lips and down my neck.

Was she still in the towel or had she let it fall to the floor?

I envisioned her slowly trailing her fingertips down the curve of her breast before settling between her thighs. With a subtle shift, she parted her legs ever so slightly and her fingers slid in effortlessly, finding her desire for me.

I tightened my fist around my cock as I thrust into it,

wanting more and more of her. Every touch, every stroke brought me closer to the edge.

I could feel my release building inside me, and I could almost hear her moans as if she were close too. The image of us together consumed me; our bodies intertwined as we reached the peak of pleasure together.

I quickened my pace, imagining that she was doing the same, our hands moving in sync as we rode out our orgasms.

"Fuck." I squeezed harder and pumped faster as I thought of her watching me.

Verena was mine. She was mine. I didn't care whether she knew it or not.

It was my only thought as I came, my body convulsing with pleasure. "Verena." Her name slipped from my lips, louder than I should have allowed, but I couldn't stop it.

The sound of the water hitting the tiles was the only noise as I tried to catch my breath. I leaned against the wall, and my eyes fluttered shut as I imagined her doing the same.

After a few moments, I straightened up and turned off the water. I reached for the towel on the rack, my hands shaking slightly as I wiped the water from my face. I couldn't stop thinking about her, about the way her skin felt beneath mine.

About the way I wanted to give her the world when I couldn't even offer her safety.

I quickly toweled off and attempted to compose myself, even though I was still aching for her touch, and I looked at the base of the door just as I saw her shadow disappear.

CHAPTER 17
VERENA

The soft morning light filtered through the window, casting a warm glow upon the room. The dust particles floated in the beams, creating a delicate dance as they twirled and swirled in the air.

I ran my fingers through my tangled hair, feeling the dampness of sweat on my skin. The sheet clung to me uncomfortably in the heat of the room, and I attempted to kick it off.

But it wouldn't budge.

A low groan escaped my lips as I attempted to shift my position, only to be met with a firm grip tightening around my waist.

Dacre.

His warm breath tickled the back of my neck as he nuzzled closer. I could feel the steady rise and fall of his chest against my back, a comforting rhythm that matched the beat of my heart.

With each inhale and exhale, he seemed to draw me closer, the heat emanating from his body enveloped me, wrapping me in warmth and desire.

Last night, I had pretended to be asleep once he finally emerged from the bathroom and stumbled back into the cramped bedroom. With only one bed in the room, there was no escape for either of us. And after hearing him groan my name through the closed door as he bathed, I couldn't bring myself to face him.

If I had, I would have begged him to show me what he had been doing, begged him to touch me until this ache that seemed to overtake my body would disappear.

My heart raced as I faced back toward the window. I didn't want to move. I didn't want to wake him.

But heat erupted across my skin, a desperation for him that I couldn't control.

I pressed my back against his chest, and I could feel his erection pressed against my ass. I shouldn't have wanted to stay there. I should have been running as far away from him as I could get.

But I didn't want to.

He had managed to secure me passage onto one of those ships I saw in the harbor. He got *us* passage, and as much as I wanted to pretend like that didn't matter, it did.

He was planning to leave this kingdom with me, leave the rebellion and Wren.

My chest ached as I thought of her, thought of how badly she would hate me if I took her brother from her, how badly she probably already did.

My mind couldn't fathom the consequences he would

face if he were to return to the hidden city. He had chosen me over the rebellion. He turned his back on them the moment he wouldn't give me up, and I could still feel the fear coursing through me as I watched his father try to beat the truth from his lips.

He shifted behind me, his arm tightening against my stomach as his nose brushed against the back of my neck.

Get up, Verena.

Leave him.

But I hesitated.

I hesitated, caught between the pull to disentangle myself from his embrace and the overwhelming desire to stay there forever. My body shifted uneasily, muscles coiled with indecision, but he held fast with a firmness that sent shivers down my spine.

"Let me go," I whispered, my voice still heavy with sleep.

"Not yet." His breath was warm on my skin as he inhaled deeply, savoring the scent. Then, with gentle pressure, he pressed his lips against the nape of my neck. A slow, tender caress. Each movement of his lips seemed to trace every curve and contour of my neck as if he wanted to commit it to memory with each touch.

His hand moved gently on my stomach, his fingers tracing delicate patterns against my skin. My body reacted instinctively, tensing under his touch. I tried to control my breathing, but it quickened in response to the electricity coursing through me.

My legs pressed together in a futile attempt to suppress

the growing ache between them, but it only seemed to intensify with each passing moment.

My body was betraying me, responding to his touch despite knowing that I shouldn't.

"I-I need to go," I stuttered, my voice shaking with emotion.

He didn't say anything for a moment, and my heart raced with anticipation.

But then he spoke, his voice soft yet commanding. "Go where, Verena?"

I swallowed hard and didn't dare look back at him. If I did, I feared what I would do.

His fingers were still trailing over my stomach, his touch like a ghost of an embrace, and it made me feral.

I leaned back into him, my body melting against his with an almost imperceptible movement. His presence behind me was palpable, the heat of his skin searing through my clothes. My heart raced as I pressed closer to him and felt the hard length of his arousal against my ass.

A shiver ran down my spine, and I couldn't resist the urge to move, ever so slightly, in search of that delicious friction. And he responded with a deep, primal groan that sent a rush of heat through me.

His teeth grazed against my shoulder and gave me the fuel I needed to press back harder against him.

"Fuck." The word was lost against my skin as his fingers moved to the edge of my undergarments.

He ran one finger beneath, teasing the fabric, teasing me, and I arched into him.

My eyes fluttered shut as he continued his torturous touch, my body responding without hesitation. I couldn't deny the desire coursing through me, the need for his touch overwhelming any rational thought.

His lips trailed down my neck, his breath hot against my skin, and I let out a soft moan. He took that as encouragement, another finger slipping beneath the edge of the fabric and brushing against my hot skin.

My body trembled in response, every nerve on fire.

I let my fingers trail over his, pushing them down more firmly, begging him with my body for what I wanted instead of my words.

But he held firm where he was.

His touch was slow and soft, and it was fucking torture.

I whimpered as I tried to guide his hand lower again, but he didn't allow me to.

"What do you want?" This time there was no softness to his voice. His question was a demand.

One that I had no intention of answering.

I pushed back against him, my body still hungry for his touch, and let out a frustrated groan when he didn't give in. But then his hand moved away completely, leaving me cold and empty.

"Use your words."

I turned around to face him, my eyes flashing with anger and need. "You know what I want, Dacre."

"Then tell me." His hand moved back to my stomach, and I tensed as he slid his fingers back beneath my undergarments. Lower than they had been before but still so far from where I needed them.

I groaned and pushed my body harder against him, grinding against his arousal in search of release.

The comforting warmth of his body pressed against mine was suddenly replaced by the cool, crisp feel of the sheets beneath me. I turned my head to see him shifting behind me, the angles and curves of his silhouette highlighted by the soft rays of sunlight streaming in through the window. With a deep sigh, he slowly rose out of the bed.

"What are you doing?" I asked, my voice trembling, as if afraid to break the spell that had enveloped us moments before.

I watched the muscles in his back tense as he grabbed his shirt and slipped it over his shoulders. He turned to face me as he began buttoning it up, and he was still so incredibly hard. "I need to go back down to the docks and confirm that everything is good for tomorrow."

"After that?" I laughed, the sound bitter and desperate.

"After what, exactly?" He reached for his pants as he watched me, waiting for me to talk.

"You're such an ass." I reached for the sheet as I sat up in the small bed, wrapping it around my chest as if it would protect me.

He leaned forward, his hands pressing into the bed until his face was only inches from mine. "You can call me whatever you want, but the next time I touch you, you're going to be begging me for it."

My traitorous body reacted to his words, but he was wrong.

"That will never happen."

He smirked, and the urge to lean forward and press my mouth to his was overwhelming.

"You've begged for it before." He raised one hand and tucked my hair behind my ear before I slapped it away. "You were so fucking wet when you begged for it then. What do you think I would find now if I had lowered my hand like you wanted me to?"

I pressed my thighs together but didn't answer him. We both knew the answer without me having to speak a word, and that only pissed me off more.

"You don't trust me." He searched my eyes. "I'm only going to touch you when you're sure that you want it, when you're sure that you want me."

He stood, leaving me alone in the bed, a mix of lust and anger still coursing through me. He turned his back to me before sitting down on the bed and pulling his pants up his legs. He was leaving me again, leaving me alone and so damn frustrated, and I refused to let it happen. Even though it was irrational, I refused.

I stood from the bed, dropping the sheet to the floor, as I moved through the room. I grabbed the new clothes from the desk where I had placed them the night before. I gripped the hem of my thin nightshirt before I jerked it over my head and reached for the new shirt he had bought me.

The soft rustle of sheets filled the room as Dacre shifted on the bed behind me. I could feel his intense gaze burning into my back as I quickly dressed, trying to ignore the burning heat that coursed through my body.

"What are you doing?"

"Going to the docks, apparently." I stepped into the pants, so much softer than the leathers I had been wearing.

"No. You're not," Dacre growled, and I heard him stand as I tucked in my shirt.

"If you are, then I am too." I was being irrational, but he had forced me to be this way. I was angry and feeling so damn needy.

And he refused to meet those needs.

"It's not safe for you to leave this room, Verena."

"It's not safe for me in the room either." I turned toward him and crossed my arms. Gods, was he this handsome earlier?

"You're not leaving this room." His voice left no room for argument, but still I argued.

"Don't do that. Don't cage me like him." My words were harsh and bitter, and I regretted them the moment they left my lips.

His eyes narrowed before he stepped forward and grabbed a thin blanket off the back of the chair. He lifted it in his hands, folding it neatly before he lifted it over my head like a shroud, the soft fabric draping over my hair and neck.

"To protect you from the brutal sun." He wrapped the tail end of the blanket over my lower face, obscuring my features. "Like many of the sailors wear."

I nodded even as my hands trembled.

"Verena." He said my name so softly and I looked up at him, desperate for anything he would tell me. "I'll never forgive you if you get caught."

You. Not us.

It was my safety that hung in the balance.

My safety that weighed heavily on his mind as he opened the door and led me from the room.

CHAPTER 18
DACRE

A s soon as our feet hit the cobblestone street, my senses went on high alert. Every sound was amplified, every scent overwhelming.

I mentally scolded myself for not refusing Verena's request to leave. I should have kept her safe within the confines of the inn, should have tied her ass to the chair until she had no choice but to stay.

But the way she had looked at me cut through my chest like a razor. Her words comparing me to her father's suffocating control, twisted around my mind.

It was suffocating, drowning me in overwhelming guilt for letting her come as we strode side by side toward the docks.

As we stepped onto the main street, a cacophony of people and energy surrounded us. I instinctively pulled Verena closer to me, feeling her body tense against mine.

The tension in her body was palpable, a result that we were both at fault for.

Even though I knew she probably only blamed me.

But I wasn't lying when I told her that I wasn't going to give in to her until she begged me. I refused to be a mere escape for her, a fleeting moment of pleasure that she could find with anyone else.

I wanted her to crave me because it was my touch, my presence, that she yearned for with every fiber of her being. Just as I ached for her in return.

I wanted there to be no fear in her eyes when she looked at me, no distrust.

I had seen no signs of my father or his men since arriving at the southern coast, but my eyes scanned the horizon for any sign of them. Despite the lack of physical evidence that they were here, the constant anticipation and deep-rooted distrust for my own flesh and blood weighed heavily on me.

I didn't know the extent of the injuries I had inflicted upon them as we escaped, the damage I had caused and how far behind I had left them. The internal conflict raged within me, hoping that my actions were enough to prevent them from catching up. But no matter what happened between us, he was still my father.

He had great plans for our kingdom once upon a time, but now those plans came at the cost of Verena. He had spoken of her as if she were nothing more than a piece of meat to be used as bait to lure her father into submission.

She was a price that he was more than willing to pay, a sacrifice that cost him nothing.

And I would never forgive him for it.

The very thought of leaving our kingdom made my stomach turn, but I would do whatever it took to protect her.

Yet, despite my resolve, thoughts of Wren and Kai still lingered in the back of my mind. I forced myself to push them away, to banish them so far that they could no longer cloud my judgment. Their presence only served to sow seeds of doubt and hesitation within me.

And I couldn't afford either. Neither of us could.

As we neared the chaotic harbor, Verena turned to me and asked, her voice uneasy, "Which way are we going?"

I raised my hand to point toward the right, where a large wooden ship was docked. Its towering mast reached up toward the cloudless sky, and the bustle of men loading cargo onto its massive deck filled the air with shouts and clanging metal.

The scent of salt water and fish wafted through the salty breeze, tinged with the underlying smell of sweat.

Verena seemed to take it all in as the unforgiving wind whipped at her makeshift scarf. It tugged at the edges, trying to pull free and expose her to the prying eyes around us.

"You stay at my side," I urged her, trying to keep my tone low and calm. "And don't speak unless you absolutely have to. We don't need to draw any attention to us."

Verena nodded silently, though her clenched jaw and narrowed eyes betrayed her frustration at being relegated to a mere bystander in this dangerous game.

But I couldn't afford for her to be reckless or for

someone to question who she was right now; her safety was my main concern. It didn't matter if her ego was bruised in the process. All that mattered was getting her out of here in one piece.

The pungent scent of fish overwhelmed us as we stepped onto the docks. Sailors gutted and cleaned various sea creatures, their tools and discarded remnants scattered haphazardly around them.

Amid the flurry of bodies, we pushed our way through the crowd toward the ship I had secured passage on for Verena and myself. My heart raced as we climbed aboard, my grip on her hand tightening with each step.

I searched for the familiar face of the captain I had spoken with just yesterday, my eyes darting across the busy deck, and the sound of waves crashing against the hull filled my ears as we made our way deeper onto the ship.

Minutes passed before the captain finally emerged from below deck, his gruff voice barking orders at the crew. He stopped in front of us, eyeing me warily before turning his attention to Verena.

"Ah, this must be her, the one you are trying to escape with." Despite the chaos around us, his voice cut through the noise like a sharp knife, carrying its gruff and authoritative tone with ease.

Escape. The word hung heavily in the air, echoing in my mind as he looked her over with a steely gaze.

I never used that word with him, but I guessed that a man desperate enough to pay all of his coins and his mother's dagger was easy enough to spot.

We were escaping.

The captain's scrutinizing gaze made me shift uncomfortably, my hand tightening around Verena's as I tried to remain calm and composed.

"We're just checking in," I confirmed, keeping my tone steady despite the nerves hammering in my stomach. "We wanted to make sure everything is settled for tomorrow for the both of us."

The captain raised an eyebrow before grunting in acknowledgment. "Everything is as planned." His rough hand patted my dagger at his side, and I watched as Verena's eyes followed the movement. She stared intently at the weapon, and my unease grew with each passing moment.

"We shall leave with the dawn," he said, casting a stern glance between us. "We will leave without you if you aren't here."

"We'll be here," I reassured him, clasping Verena's slender hand tighter in mine. I could feel her pulse quicken under my touch, and I knew she shared my discomfort with the captain's scrutiny.

I hated the way he was staring her down, as if trying to decode all of her secrets. His gaze held a sharpness that made me want to step in front of Verena and protect her from whatever he was thinking.

But I knew we needed him for our plan to succeed. So I swallowed my discomfort, even as dread settled in my stomach like a heavy stone.

I took a step back, pulling her with me, and nodded my head to the captain. We stepped off the ship, the vessel that would take us away from it all, and the salty sea air filled my lungs as I guided us back toward the familiar inn.

Despite the constant knot of uncertainty that weighed heavy in my stomach, I had just enough coins left to pay the innkeeper for another hot meal. The thought of returning to the warm comfort and familiar safety of our room brought a wave of relief and hope amid the chaos that surrounded us.

Tonight we would be safe, and tomorrow, I looked behind me at the ship once more, we would sail away from this kingdom without looking back.

As we walked, Verena suddenly grabbed my hand with a force that made me stop in my tracks. I turned to face her, my brow furrowing in concern.

"What's wrong?" I asked, observing the tension in her body and the way she anxiously bit on her bottom lip.

"Nothing." She shook her head before stealing a glance behind her at the vast expanse of the sea. "Can we…" She hesitated before taking a deep breath and asking, "Can we go to the ocean?"

"We'll be on the ocean tomorrow." There was no telling how many days we would spend on the sea before we reached the next kingdom.

"That's not what I mean." She looked back at me. "I want to feel the salt on my skin and the waves crashing against my legs," she continued, her eyes pleading with me.

The vast expanse of the ocean stretched out before us, its waves crashing against the rocky shore below.

"It's not safe for us to stay out here," I murmured, glancing over my shoulder to make sure no one was watching us.

Verena's eyes were fixed on the endless horizon, her voice filled with longing and desperation. "I've been able to see the ocean outside my window my whole life, but I've never been in it."

"You felt the salt water on your skin in the hidden city," I replied, trying to reason with her.

"That's different and you know it."

"Verena," I sighed and shook my head, before scanning our surroundings once more. We weren't safe.

"Please," she pleaded, wrapping her hand around my forearm with a tight grip.

My heart ached as I thought about all that she had missed out on in her life, how caged she had been.

"We can't stay long."

Her face lit up, and I could see the relief wash over her.

We made our way down the rocky shore, and I helped her over a few of the large rocks.

I led us far enough down where no one would notice us, far enough away that no one would notice *her*.

I sat on one of the rocks and watched as she removed her boots and rolled up her pants before standing at the edge of the water. She hesitated for a moment, looking at the cold, blue water before taking a deep breath and stepping into the waves.

She stepped in farther, letting the waves wash over her calves, and she laughed as the water lapped at her legs.

She turned to me, her eyes shining with gratitude. "Thank you."

I smiled back at her and nodded, mesmerized by how

the entire coast was before me but all I could see was her. "You're welcome."

She moved in a bit farther until the waves hit her knees, soaking her pants.

As she tilted her face toward the sun, I couldn't help but notice the way the light danced across her skin, creating a soft glow around her features. A gentle breeze playfully danced against the delicate fabric of her scarf, causing it to flutter and sway behind her like a graceful ribbon caught in the wind.

I leaned back on my hands as I watched her. "Is it cold?" I asked, my voice barely above a whisper.

"Come and find out," she replied with a mischievous grin on her lips. She turned to face me fully, and I was struck once again by how stunning she was.

"I'm fine," I said, shaking my head, more than content just to watch her, captivated by her every move.

She playfully splashed the water in my direction, her laughter carrying on the wind.

"Verena!" I couldn't help but laugh along with her as the water caught me by surprise.

"Get in," she urged, kicking the water with a mischievous glint in her eye.

I watched her, a warm feeling spreading through my chest at the sight of her.

I couldn't resist her any longer, and I kicked off my boots with a grin as I stood up and made my way toward her.

The water was cold against my skin, sending shivers through my body as I waded closer to her. Each wave crashed against my legs, the salty spray mingling with the coolness of the water. I could feel the sand shifting beneath my feet, creating a soothing rhythm with each step I took.

She squealed as I scooped her up in my arms and carried her toward the deeper waters.

"Hey!" she protested, splashing me as we went.

We reached a spot where the water was just above our waists, and I sank down into the water, taking her with me.

Verena laughed as the waves crashed against us, the salt water stinging my eyes as it sprayed me in the face.

I laughed alongside her, but I didn't let her go. She had her arms wrapped around my shoulders as she kicked her feet in the water, and I was overwhelmed by how free she looked in that moment.

"I used to wish I was a mermaid." She kicked again before closing her eyes and leaning her head back until the sun's rays kissed her face.

"Why a mermaid?" I chuckled softly, my eyes roaming over every curve and angle of her delicate features. Her skin glowed in the soft light, highlighting the subtle freckles dusted across her cheeks. Her lips curved in a playful smile, revealing a dimple on one side.

"Can you imagine how free they must be?" She let her arms fall from my neck, holding them out at her sides in the water, and I held her weight in my arms.

"You'll be free soon." I stared down at her, watching her expression as the smile slipped from her lips.

"I'll never be free." With a slow, deliberate movement, she opened her eyes and looked up at me. Her gaze held a depth of emotion that made my chest ache.

"Yes, you will." I nodded. "I won't stop until you are."

She slipped gracefully out of my hold and brushed the water from her face. She turned toward the horizon, the wind gently whipping around us as she took in the vast view before us.

"Was that your dagger the captain had at his side?" Her question sliced through the air like a blade, catching me off guard.

"Technically, it was my mother's."

She turned, her gaze slamming into mine. "You gave him your mother's dagger?"

I hesitated, unsure of how to respond. "I didn't have much of a choice."

Verena took a deep breath and let it out slowly, her eyes locked on mine. "You shouldn't have."

"I would have given him anything he asked for."

We stood there, the weight of our pasts and the uncertainty of our futures crashing into us with each wave.

"You're going to regret leaving," Verena said suddenly, breaking the quiet moment between us.

Her words hung in the air, heavy with a warning that I wouldn't heed.

"I regret so many things, Verena, but leaving this world for you won't be one of them."

She turned away from me, emotion clouding her face that she didn't want me to see. "We should head back."

"We should." I reached for her, catching her hand in mine under the water.

She looked back at me, her eyes clashing with mine,

and in that moment, I knew that every word I had spoken was true. Nothing would make me regret her.

CHAPTER 19
VERENA

W e were still dripping wet by the time we made it back to the inn.

Dacre approached the wooden desk, his hand reaching into his pocket to retrieve a few shiny coins. He slid them across the worn surface to the innkeeper, requesting food to be brought up to our room. My stomach growled with hunger, but it paled in comparison to the insatiable desire building within me for him.

I wrapped my arms around my chest, trying to ward off the cool air bleeding through my wet clothes as I anxiously waited for Dacre to open the door.

As soon as he did, we both eagerly kicked off our boots, the sound of their thuds echoing through the empty room.

Dacre strode across the room with purpose, his wet footsteps leaving a trail of water on the floor. He disappeared into the bathroom, and after a moment, emerged with one towel in hand while he pressed the other against the nape of his neck.

Water trickled down his tousled hair as I reached for the towel he offered. The fabric was soft as I pressed it against me.

"You can have the bathroom to change," he said, his eyes lingering on my mouth as he spoke.

Heat simmered under my skin, erupting until it spread through my whole body.

"Thank you," I managed to say as I nodded, but I didn't move. I just stood there staring at him the same way he was staring at me.

He took a step closer, his hand reaching out to gently sweep a stray strand of hair from my face. I shivered at the touch of his cool fingers against my burning skin.

In that moment, all the doubts and fears that had plagued my mind seemed to fade away, like a thick fog dissipating under the warm rays of the sun.

The betrayal that had been consuming me since the moment he sent me on the run now seemed to crumble into weak and insignificant fragments.

I wanted him. Gods, I needed him.

"Go, Verena." His voice was low and rough, sending shivers down my spine. He nodded toward the bathroom as he slid his hand down the side of my neck, his touch electrifying.

I nodded slowly, my eyes locked on his in a silent plea, but I still didn't move.

Dacre's fingers tangled in my wet hair, pulling me even

closer to him. Our faces were inches apart, the rush of our breaths mingling in the space between us.

"Verena," he practically growled my name, his gaze moving from my lips to meet my eyes. "You need to go before I do something that you don't want me to."

A sharp inhale escaped my lips, and I could feel the rapid thumping of my pulse beneath his fingers as if it were trying to burst out of my skin. "And what if it is what I want?"

Every nerve in my body seemed to tingle with anticipation as I waited for his next move.

His hand slid around the nape of my neck, his grip firm yet gentle. The warmth of his palm seeped into my skin, sending sparks of electricity through my body. I felt a soft fire ignite within me, warming me from the inside out.

My body instinctively leaned toward him, my muscles relaxing under the soothing pressure of his touch.

"Then you need to tell me, Verena." His eyes seemed to sear into mine, and I could feel the weight of his conflicted emotions, yet his fingers never faltered in their hold on me. "I wasn't lying to you before. I won't touch you unless you want me to."

My heart pounded in my chest, a wild and unruly beast clawing at the confines of my rib cage, yearning for his touch.

"I need…I need you."

The words were like a plea. They clawed at my throat, begging to be heard.

Dacre's eyes flared and blurred the world around me as his breathing grew heavy and erratic against my skin. He leaned closer to me until his lips brushed against the shell of my ear.

His words were like a caress as they passed over my skin. "But do you want me?" he whispered, his lips moving against my skin.

I nodded, unable to form the words he needed to hear.

He pulled back slightly, his hand tightening on the back of my neck. "I need your words, Verena." His voice was filled with longing. "I need to know that this is what you want."

Without hesitation, I spoke the only truth I had. "I want you."

With those three simple words, everything changed.

Dacre's lips crashed onto mine with an urgency and desperation I had never felt before. His teeth grazed over my bottom lip, sending shivers down my spine. A low, guttural groan escaped from his throat as I eagerly parted my lips to taste more of him.

His fingers traced a path from my neck down to my hips, exploring every curve and dip of my body. With a strong yet gentle touch, he lifted me, and I instinctively wrapped my arms around his broad shoulders.

Our bodies molded together as he carried us toward the bed, never breaking our kiss.

He lowered me onto the plush bed, and I let out a small laugh as I bounced lightly on the mattress. But my laughter was cut short when I looked up at Dacre and saw the intense, almost predatory glint in his eyes.

My fingers brushed over his chest, feeling the taut muscles beneath his damp shirt. He caught my hand in his and brought it to his lips, placing a gentle kiss on my skin.

"Gods, you're beautiful." He leaned forward, lifting my damp shirt until it rested below my breasts. With a feather-light touch, he ran his nose along my stomach before pressing his lips to the sensitive skin just below my belly button.

A sharp gasp escaped my lips as his warm breath tickled my skin. A shiver of pleasure rippled through my body as his lips trailed lower and lower, creating a trail of fire in its wake.

My hands tangled in his hair as I moaned his name, my body arching toward him in need.

His strong, calloused hands roamed over every inch of my body, eliciting shivers and gasps from me. As he made his way back up to my lips, our bodies pressed tightly together, creating a heat and electricity between us that was almost tangible.

The kiss grew in intensity with each passing second, our lips moving together as desire coursed through our veins. I pushed my hips against his, our bodies grinding together as we both yearned for more.

He leaned back, positioning himself between my parted thighs and trailing his hand down my body in a slow caress.

"I have been tortured with dreams of touching you again," he murmured, his voice low and husky with desire. "I've been tortured by the memories of the first time." As our eyes met, his intense gaze bore into me like a searing flame, the heat almost suffocating, yet I couldn't look away. "Haunted by thoughts of what I should have done, of the way I should have worshipped you."

A wildfire spread across my skin as he traced delicate patterns along my curves until he reached the top of my pants.

"I should have fallen to my knees for you as I will do now."

I could feel the intensity of his longing in the way his fingers trembled against my flesh, a fire within me that threatened to consume us both.

My breath hitched in my throat as I felt his warm fingers deftly unbuttoning my trousers, releasing a flurry of nerves that had been coiled deep inside me.

"Dacre," I whispered, my voice barely above a breath as his skilled fingers danced along my skin, sending shivers coursing through me.

"Like salt in the sea, you have become ingrained in every part of me, and I have been drowning in my regrets."

I shook my head because I didn't want his words, my chest felt as if it were caving in as he spoke them, but he wouldn't stop.

"You should send me away, Verena. Banish me from ever touching you again. I don't deserve you after everything I've done."

"Stop." My voice shook with the desperate command.

"Your entire existence has been dedicated to preparing for your place as ruler of our kingdom, yet you have never been revered. It is a privilege I am unworthy of, but I would surrender every breath to worship you if only you would grant me the honor."

His words cut through me, crashing into me in wave after wave until I felt like I couldn't breathe. I reached up and touched his face, my fingers brushing against the stubble on his jaw.

"Dacre, please."

His dark eyes flared as he gripped my hand in his and pressed his lips to my palm.

"I am devoted to you." His intense gaze locked with mine. "Please let me fall to my knees before you and prove my devotion with my tongue against your skin."

My breath caught at his words and I nodded eagerly, desperation for him pulsing through every inch of me.

"I am desperate to taste you." With one swift movement, he yanked my pants down my hips, the once tender touch now replaced with one of urgency.

He lowered his head, his teeth grazing my skin as he trailed hot kisses along the sensitive flesh of my bare thighs. My body arched, my hips instinctively bucking toward him, yearning for more.

With a quick flick of his wrist, he removed my pants completely before tossing them on the floor and leaving me bare in front of him.

The urge to hide my body was overwhelming. But Dacre had already seen the worst of my scars, and as he hooked his hands beneath both of my knees, that feeling faded. He spread my legs apart and pinned them down on either side of the mattress.

He lowered himself down, his warm breath caressing my inner thigh as his tongue traced the delicate seam between my thigh and my pussy. A surge of pleasure shot through me, causing my hips to buck off the bed and eagerly chase his mouth.

He slid both of his arms beneath my legs as he settled under my thighs, on his knees, and the heat from his hands seared into my skin as he spread me open before him.

With a slow, deliberate movement, he ran his tongue through me, making my body convulse and causing me to call out his name.

His deep growl against me only added fuel to the fire, and I couldn't help but dig my fingers into his hair as he worked me with his mouth.

"So fucking wet," he breathed, his words vibrating against me. "Is this all for me?"

"You know it is." I pressed my head back against the mattress as I tried to close my legs around him.

"Show me, Verena," he commanded, with a hint of desperation in his voice. "Fuck my mouth and show me how badly you want me to be the only one who worships at your feet."

A whimper left my lips as I did as he said. I moved my hips against his mouth, chasing the waves of pleasure that were crashing over me.

His hands found their way to my ass, lifting me and anchoring me against his mouth as he sucked my clit between his lips.

"Fuck," I moaned and pulled on his hair, trying to get him impossibly closer to me.

Dacre grasped my ass, jerking me down to the edge of the bed, still working me with his mouth.

"Dacre, I'm so close," I gasped.

He increased his pressure, his lips sucking and pulling at my sensitive flesh as he slid a finger inside me.

I felt reckless with him between my thighs, completely and utterly out of control.

"Look at me."

I could feel my orgasm approaching, and I buried my head back against the mattress.

"Now, Verena."

My eyes snapped open, and my gaze met his, unable to deny his command. "I want to taste your cum. I can't go another moment without tasting your pleasure and knowing that it belongs to no one but me."

I called out his name, my body arching off the bed as I did just as he said and came against his mouth.

Dacre held me tight, not stopping until I was spent, kissing me softly along my hip bone.

I sank down onto the soft mattress as he stood. Without hesitation, he flipped me over until my chest was firmly pressed against the smooth fabric. His strength and control evident in his every move when I felt like I had none.

His fingers traced a tantalizing path down my spine, sending shivers of pleasure through every nerve in my body. They then moved over my ass, gently caressing and exploring until they finally reached the warm, slick wetness between my thighs. I couldn't help but moan at his touch, my body arching toward him, somehow still desperate for more.

With a possessive growl, Dacre thrust two fingers inside me, stretching me in a way that had me panting and begging. His other hand reached around me, his thumb skillfully brushing against my sensitive clit.

"Dacre, please," I begged, writhing beneath him as he tortured me with his touch.

He paused, his fingers still embedded deep within me, and his warm breath caressed the back of my neck. "Tell me what you want."

"Fuck me," I whimpered.

"You are mine, Verena," he growled. "You belong to me." His words sent a rush of wetness between my legs, and I couldn't help but arch my back, offering myself to him completely.

"Tell me you are mine." His words were a low, pleading growl that reverberated through the air.

I could hear him behind me, the rustle of fabric as he removed his clothes.

He positioned himself between my legs, his hard length pressing against me. He ran himself back and forth through my wetness, and I jerked when he hit my clit.

"Tell me, Verena," he demanded again, his voice rough with need. His breath tickled my neck as he leaned over me, and I dug my fingers into the sheets as his heartbeat pounded against my back.

"I'm yours."

Dacre groaned, his hips thrusting forward, rubbing against me. His fingers slid from my wetness, and I felt him position the head of his cock against my entrance.

I rocked back against him. "Please, Dacre."

My body trembled as he began to slide in, filling me

with every inch. I gasped, my grip tightening on the sheets, as he slowly buried himself inside me.

His hips moved in a slow rhythm, pulling back and then thrusting forward, each movement sending waves of pleasure coursing through me.

He leaned forward, his lips brushing against the back of my neck, his breath warm against my skin. "You feel so damn good."

The weight of his body left mine as he leaned back, his hand roaming over my ass before his fingers tangled with the hem of my still-damp shirt. He pushed it higher, exposing my bare skin to him, and I stilled when I felt him falter.

My scars.

I wanted to stop him, to pull my shirt back down and hide from him, but his fingers were already grazing over the jagged scars that littered my back.

"Dacre." My voice trembled, and I wanted to beg him to stop. It was too much.

"I will never let anyone hurt you again." He promised something that he would never be able to honor, but his oath burned through me as if he had branded it within my veins. "The king will never touch you again."

His lips traced over my scars with gentle precision, as if trying to erase the lingering pain that still haunted me even though they had become nothing more than marks on my skin.

"Mine," he whispered hoarsely, that one simple word a promise.

He slid one hand under my body, gently pressing

against my chest before lifting me up. My back arched against his firm chest as he pulled me close. His knees settled between mine, anchoring us together, as he wrapped his arms around me and held me against him.

He felt impossibly deep inside me as his thrusts grew harder and more urgent. I let out a low moan as he possessively wrapped his hand around my neck, holding me close as his body moved against mine.

"Look at me, Verena," he whispered, and I was startled by how gentle his words were.

I turned and looked at him over my shoulder, his lips eagerly met mine. The intensity of his touch caused my body to quiver and shake as he slowly slid in and out of me.

I was utterly consumed by him, and my fingers dug into his, trying to pull him impossibly closer.

"I'm sorry, Verena." His apology was a mere murmur against my lips, barely audible over the pounding of my heart. Slowly, he pulled me away from him, his intense gaze locking with mine. In his eyes, I saw a tumultuous mix of guilt, regret, and longing. "I'm so fucking sorry."

"Please, Dacre," I begged as a wave of emotions crashed over me, threatening to pull me under. "I need you."

A deep moan escaped his lips as he thrust harder and deeper inside me. His fingers tightened around my neck, pulling me closer to him as he kissed me with an intensity that stole my breath.

His other hand moved down my body, tracing every curve and dip before he pressed his fingers against my sensitive clit. I jerked forward just as his next words crashed into me.

"I am yours, Verena," he growled against my mouth. "In this kingdom and the next, wherever the tides take you, I am yours."

I swallowed, my heart racing in my chest as I felt completely vulnerable and exposed to him.

I let him claim me, let him take whatever it was he needed from me as I did the same with him, and when I came again, it was with his name on my lips.

He picked up the pace, his thrusts becoming more desperate, more unrelenting. My cries echoed in the room as he took me, possessing me completely.

With a loud groan, Dacre surrendered to his pleasure, burying himself deep inside me one final time. I felt the warmth of his release inside me as I tried to catch my breath.

We stayed like that, my body spent while he held me up against him, and he pressed his lips against my neck and shoulder over and over as if he hadn't gotten his fill.

Slowly, he pulled out of me, and I felt a small pang of loss at the emptiness inside me.

Dacre rolled me over until I was facing him again, and he lifted my hand and pressed his lips to my fingers.

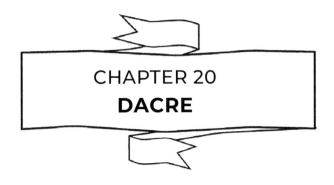

CHAPTER 20
DACRE

Thick steam filled the bathroom as Verena stepped inside. The hot, damp air was clinging to my skin as I reached for her hand, and she took it without hesitation.

I held on to her as she stepped into the bath, and she groaned as she sank down into the heat of the water.

Her eyes met mine as she looked up, her focus on me alone, and the vulnerability in her expression brought an ache to my chest.

Softly, she reached out, her fingers grazing my own. "Get in with me."

I hesitated for only a second because I wanted to take care of her. "Are you sure?"

She nodded, and I took a deep breath and stepped into the bath. The hot water enveloped me as I sank down behind her, her body settling perfectly between my thighs, my arm draped around her shoulders as she leaned into me.

We sat in silence for a while, just the soft splash of the

water filling the air as I cupped some in my hands and let it fall over her shoulders.

"I used to love baths when I was little," she murmured as she leaned her head back against my shoulder, seeming to savor the way the water trailed over her body.

"I hated them." I chuckled and a soft, wistful smile tugged at the corners of her lips as she looked up at me.

"I bet you were a handful as a boy," she teased.

"I was worse than a handful. My mother nearly had a heart attack daily because of my mischief, and Wren was so well-behaved in comparison." The thought of my sister brought a pang to my chest, but I forced it away.

"I could see that." She nodded, her eyes filled with amusement. "Wren has always seemed much more level-headed than you."

"There was this one time when I ventured farther into the hidden city than I had ever been before, despite being strictly forbidden to do so. I ended up lost for hours, and when my mother finally found me, she was beside herself with worry while Wren just smirked at me." I laughed, tracing my finger gently down the slope of her neck. "She, of course, was with me when my exploration started, but left me the moment she told me that we should turn around and I refused."

Verena blinked up at me, her expression soft. "You should learn to listen to her."

"I have." I nodded earnestly. "I've gotten much better at it since then."

A small crease appeared between her eyebrows as she averted her gaze from me. "What did Wren say about me?"

"It was hard to remember exactly," I admitted. "She was too busy slamming her hands into my chest." I absent-mindedly rubbed at the spot as Verena turned her attention back to me. "But I think it was along the lines of she was going to kill me if I didn't find you, murder me if I let my father find you first."

Verena shuddered against me. "I wish I hadn't lied to her." She shook her head. "She was the first real friend I've ever had."

My chest ached at her words. She wasn't saying them for pity. They were simply the truth, and I hated that even more.

"You didn't have any friends in the palace?"

She sighed, her eyes losing their luster. "I had people, servants, but my father kept me away from anyone who would realize I was powerless."

I furrowed my brow, trying to understand her pain.

"I had a lady's maid who bathed me, dressed me, and brought me food. She was with me the most after my mother died, and she never left the palace." She sighed, resting her head on my shoulder once more.

"Our kingdom was already in unrest. Our people would have rejected your right to the throne even more if they knew you possessed no magic," I spoke out loud, trying to make sense of what her father had done.

Verena nodded, and I squeezed her tightly, feeling her body tremble against me.

"Talk of the rising rebellion only made things worse." She swallowed and looked straight ahead. "His advisers would warn him of the unrest, and he would take it out on my back with a whip. He thought he could beat the magic out of me, force it from my skin with every drop of my blood."

A storm of anger and hatred consumed me. My muscles tensed and my vision blurred as I envisioned every cruel act her father had inflicted on her, and the desire for revenge burned within me. I yearned to make him suffer in ways that mirrored the pain he had caused her. I wanted to see him grovel at her feet, pleading for mercy that would never come. But I knew deep down that none of this would bring her what she wanted, what she needed.

Freedom.

I gently cupped her face, trying to keep my voice steady. "I'm sorry, Verena."

Her eyes met mine, filled with a mixture of fear and hope. "You stopped calling me little traitor."

Her words shocked me, causing a choked laugh to fall from my lips. "I should have never called you it to begin with."

Her eyes shuttered softly, and I ran my wet fingers along her jaw. "Unless you want me to. I will call you anything you desire." I looked down just as she pressed her thighs together, almost unnoticeably.

I leaned closer to her until my mouth brushed against her ear. "Do you like being my little traitor?"

Her skin flushed a deep crimson, the color spreading from her chest to her cheeks, but she remained silent.

"Tell me, Verena. Do you enjoy being a wicked little thing?" The words dripped with desire.

She remained silent, her eyes squeezed shut and her

body trembling as she tried to catch her breath. Her chest rose and fell with each deep breath, the water gently lapping against her breasts.

She parted her legs slightly, her thighs pressing into mine in a silent invitation, and the hunger inside me surged at the sight of her, a desperate longing that made me feel like I could never quench my desire for her.

I reached forward and gripped her thighs in my hands, spreading them farther apart, and lifting them until her knees hooked over mine. Her body arched in response to the sudden movement, revealing the soft curves and dips of her body, and my cock pressed against her ass.

My fingers flexed possessively, squeezing her thighs as I whispered into her ear, "Are you wet for me again, my little traitor?"

She trembled against me as a whimper passed her lips, and she nodded her head slightly, barely grazing it against my own.

"Such a naughty little thing." I let my hand trail up her thigh, my fingers lightly grazing over the sensitive skin. She arched her body toward me, her knees pressing against mine in a desperate attempt to get closer.

But I only widened my legs, forcing her legs farther apart. Her breath quickened as she felt my touch inching closer to where she craved it most, her body trembling with anticipation.

"Please," she begged, and I ran my other hand up her chest and cupped her breast in my hand.

I ran my thumb over her nipple just as I let my fingers from my other hand trail over the seam of her pussy.

I slowly slipped my fingers between her legs, feeling the warmth and slickness that coated her. She gasped, her body tensing, and I savored the feel of her as I slid my middle finger inside.

"Tell me how it feels," I murmured, grazing my teeth over her shoulder as I pinched her nipple harder and pressed my thumb against her sensitive clit. The sensation caused her to arch her back and moan. "Do you like it when I fuck you with my fingers?" I slid a second one inside her. "Or do they make you wish it were my cock instead?" I growled, my cock throbbing at the thought.

"I want all of you," she panted, her hips bucking against my hand. "Please don't stop."

I slid my fingers in and out of her, reveling in the tightness and heat that enveloped them. With each thrust, I curled them inside her while simultaneously rubbing tiny circles on her swollen clit.

She arched her back and moaned in pleasure, her hips bucking against my hand before she reached behind her until she found my throbbing cock. As soon as her fingers wrapped around it, I felt like I was going to explode.

"Stand up," I demanded, my voice heavy with the tension that pulsed through me.

She hesitated but did just as I said, and I climbed to my knees behind her.

I ran my fingers over her ass, kneading and exploring before I slipped by hand down between her thighs from behind.

"Bend over," I instructed, "and wrap your hands around

the edge of the tub." Gods, she was so fucking wet. "You let go and I stop."

She complied, her body trembling as she bent over and held on to the edge of the bathtub. Her ass was presented to me, her pussy exposed.

"Spread for me."

She did so quickly, both of her ankles pressing against either side of the tub.

"You are so perfect," I murmured as I slid my thumbs along the seam of her pussy before spreading her open. "Such a perfect pussy that belongs to no one but me."

I leaned forward and ran my tongue through her.

Her body jerked at my touch, a low moan escaping her lips. I could taste her arousal on my tongue, and it only served to fuel my desire.

"Oh gods," she whispered, her hips swaying gently.

I continued to eat her, my tongue dipping in and out, tasting every inch of her. She moaned again as she pushed her hips back against my face.

"So fucking needy," I growled before swirling my tongue around her clit.

Her body trembled, her hips bucking slightly.

I pushed to my feet, wiping my chin with the back of my hand as I stood behind her. I caught a glimpse of myself in the fogged-up mirror above the sink. My hair was disheveled, and my skin was flushed from the hot water.

I looked like a man possessed, and I was.

I stepped out of the bathtub onto the small rug on the floor and reached for her hand. Verena straightened on shaky legs before she followed suit and climbed out with me. Her feet had barely hit the floor before I scooped her up into my arms, her legs wrapping tightly around my waist.

We moved together until she was propped against the wooden door, our bodies glistening with droplets of water.

"Watch us," I groaned as I leaned back and pressed the head of my cock against her entrance. "Don't let your eyes leave that mirror." I bit down on her neck, feeling her slick warmth envelop me as I slowly sank inside her. "I want you to see yourself come while I lose myself in you."

She moaned softly, her eyes widening as I stretched her. Her nails dug into my back as she let out the tiniest little whimper when I buried myself inside her.

She wrapped her legs tighter around me, her nails leaving crescent moons in my skin as I thrust inside her.

"That's it," I moaned as she moved her hips against mine. "Fuck me."

I kissed the side of her jaw, her eyes still glued to the two of us in the mirror, and she trembled against me as she rolled her hips.

She was sin, every part of her damning me.

I reached behind me, pulling one of her legs from around my hip and pressing my palm into her knee as I spread her open wider.

"Yes," she breathed as I hit impossibly deeper inside her.

That one word sent shock waves of pleasure through me, and I began to fuck her harder, each thrust deeper than the last. I could feel her wetness around me, slick and hot, and it drove me wild.

I gripped her ass in my other hand, pulling her closer, her walls gripping me tightly. Her head fell back, her eyes closed as she let out a low moan.

She was breathtaking.

"You're taking me so well," I said before pressing my forehead into the space between her collarbone and jaw. "The gods made you for me. Carved you from the stars themselves until I could no longer bear to gaze up at the sky without longing for you."

Her eyes, wide and unguarded, snapped to meet mine. The raw vulnerability emanating from their depths caught me off guard, stealing my breath. "Whatever comes."

I didn't know if it was a statement or a question, but I knew my answer either way. "Whatever comes, you are mine."

I needed her to feel it, to know that she truly belonged to me.

I grabbed her wrists, pinning them above her head, and thrust harder into her, twisting my hips as I did so. Her moans filled the room, her body arching against mine, her nails digging into my hand as she tried to hold on.

She was just as wild and as untamed as I was.

I leaned forward, my lips brushing against her ear as I whispered, "Come for me, love."

She arched her back and cried out, her body tightening around me as waves of pleasure washed over her. I could feel her muscles clenching around me as she hit the height of her pleasure, and with one final thrust, I let out a deep growl as I released inside her.

I stood there, leaning against her and holding her body against the door as we both panted heavily until she slowly slid down my body.

I reached behind me, fumbling for a towel, grasping the soft fabric before I carefully began cleaning her up. She shivered, and I immediately wrapped another towel around her body, shielding her from the cool air that seeped in now that we were no longer entwined.

"We need to get some sleep. Tomorrow will come before either of us is ready." I watched her carefully as I wrapped another towel around my waist, watching for any sign of regret.

But there was none.

She simply nodded before the two of us stepped out of the bathroom and back into the small room. She climbed into the bed, not worrying about clothes, and I did the same.

I quickly tucked a dagger beneath my pillow as I lay down beside her.

The room was dark, illuminated by a single candle, and she lay facing me, her arm tucked under her head.

She looked away from me, her gaze falling to the blanket between us, and I feared what was going through her mind.

I was terrified that she regretted what we'd done—that she regretted me.

"What's going through that head of yours?" I reached forward and brushed some hair out of her face.

"What?" She blinked up at me.

"You look lost in your thoughts." I swallowed and searched her eyes. "Are you okay?"

"Yes." She nodded. "Sorry. I was just thinking."

"About?" I didn't want to push her, but gods, I was desperate to know every thought that passed through her mind.

"My mom." She let out a small laugh. "That's weird, right?"

"It's not weird at all," I reassured her. "I'd love to hear about her."

Her eyes flicked over my face before falling to my chest. "She used to tell me a story every night before I went to bed."

She smiled softly, and I held my breath.

"And there was this one night where she led me through the tunnels while she was telling me a story. I thought we were having an adventure." She laughed, but the sound was sad. "I had never been in the tunnels before, never allowed to venture that far through the palace, but I think she knew I would need a way out one day."

My father had been searching for a way into the palace my whole life, searching for those tunnels.

She tugged on the blanket, pulling it over her shoulders as if it would shield her from the memories that haunted her.

"The tunnels came out right near the base of the water-fall." She pushed her hair out of her face. "There are two trees there, their roots intertwined and wound together."

She shook her head as if frustrated by her lack of recollection, but I knew the exact trees she spoke of. "I don't really remember how the story went, but it talked of magic between two people. A magic shared and molded like those trees."

"Like our magic?" I asked, the words catching in my throat. It was a topic we had avoided, and I wondered if we were both fearful of discovering the truth behind why my magic seemed to surge when she was near, why she could finally wield hers when she was by my side.

"I wasn't lying to you about my magic." She searched my eyes. "I had never felt a single stirring of power until you." She hesitated. "And I couldn't feel it in the woods, not until you found me."

My chest tightened at her admission.

"I've never felt magic like I did when you confronted my father." I licked my lips and tried to find the right words. "That's a kind of power that kings kill for, Verena. A kind of power they'd keep caged to make sure they never lose hold of it."

She blinked, apprehension creeping into her eyes.

"Verena, that is the kind of power of a queen."

Her eyes dilated, and there was so much fear staring back at me. "I don't want to be queen."

"Then you won't," I answered simply. "But you can never let your father know of your power." I clenched my hand into a fist, trying to control the sudden fear that coursed through me at the thought. "There's no telling what he'd do with it."

"He'd wreck the world." Her answer was quick as if she had been considering the options for days. "He was already capable of destroying so much with a powerless heir at his side." Her gaze darted away as if she was ashamed of who she was. "I don't want to imagine what he'd do with this."

She lifted her hand, looking down at her flesh as if she were a weapon.

I wrapped my hand around hers quickly, bringing it to my mouth.

"He won't get the chance," I reassured her. "What else do you remember from that story your mother told you? What happened to the two people whose magic melded as one?"

"A kingdom torn in blood, a world turned to ash." Her brow creased as if she couldn't remember the rest.

"But with my soul, I the worship," I finished the line for her.

The corner of her lips lifted into a smile as her eyes lit up. "But with my soul, I the worship." She snapped her fingers. "That's it."

And suddenly, it felt like a sharp blade had pierced through me. The words cut deep, leaving a searing pain in my chest and making it hard to draw breath. I could see the same look of shock on Verena's face, her features mirroring the same intense feeling coursing through her.

"Where did you learn that from?" she asked, her words quiet in the dark of the room.

"In Enveilorian," I answered, my gaze fixed on her

face. "It's a vow." The words hung in the air. "A bond between two souls in marriage."

She shook her head as if trying to make sense of my words. "I've seen weddings at the palace. I've never heard it before."

I swallowed before pressing another kiss to her knuckles. "It's reserved for mates."

CHAPTER 21
DACRE

Verena's hand trembled in mine as we made our way to the docks.

The sun had just begun its ascent over the vast ocean, casting soft hues of pink and orange across the still water. Unlike the chaotic scene we encountered the day before, the docks now felt much calmer.

I was so much calmer.

I had spent the night with Verena in my arms. But as the morning light seeped into our room, I could feel her body tense against mine. Her nervous energy radiated through the air, charged with anticipation and fear.

We were leaving everything behind—our kingdom, our families, our lives—and even though I had no regrets over my decision, a twinge of apprehension tugged at my chest.

Our escape from this kingdom was within reach, our freedom nearly tangible. The oppressive grip of both her father and mine was almost behind us, but still, a frantic panic coursed through my veins. I could feel my heart racing as we neared the port, and I knew that once we stepped foot on the ship, I could finally take a deep breath.

We walked through the quiet streets hand in hand, the same makeshift scarf from yesterday partially obscuring Verena's face, and we were just about to leave the city for the docks when I saw it.

A poster hung on a nearby building, its edges fraying in the wind. Nails punctured it and secured it to the wood.

The face of Verena was depicted with an unsettling accuracy, as if she were staring directly at me. I halted my steps, my breath catching in my throat as I took in the sight. A gasp escaped Verena's lips beside me.

In bold letters at the top of the poster read: "Reward for the Return of the Lost Princess." My eyes widened as they scanned down to the bottom where a number glinted in the light. Ten thousand gold coins were being offered for her return.

I looked over at her, studying her as I tightened the scarf around her face.

"That's my face," she whispered, her voice faltering.

"I know." I scanned the street. "Stay close to me," I warned her. "We need to get on the ship as quickly as possible."

The pressure on my chest was unbearable as we walked. Before today, most people had never seen her face. She was the princess the king hid away, the princess most people thought he was keeping safe. But now she was exposed.

I tried not to think about how many people had seen

that poster. I tried not to consider how many posters were hung throughout our kingdom.

The sounds of men preparing the ship for launch echoed off the wooden dock as we approached, and I jumped when a loud bang rang out that no one else seemed to notice.

Our footsteps resounded loudly against the worn planks, and I tried to ignore it all as I spotted the ship.

Not much farther.

Amid the crew, I spotted the captain standing on the dock, engaged in conversation with another sailor. His stern expression shifted as he caught sight of us approaching.

He exchanged a few words with his companion before heading toward us, his long strides confident and purposeful.

We met him halfway. Only a handful of steps separating us and the sea.

"You made it." The captain's voice was deep and rough. He ran his hand over his unkempt beard, a mix of salt and pepper strands protruding from his weathered face.

"I told you we'd be here." I nodded, pulling Verena closer to me until she was tucked into my side. Her warmth seeped into me, and I tried to remind myself that she was safe.

Even if I couldn't stop that nagging feeling in my gut.

"We have a couple things we need to discuss before we set sail." The captain's words tore through the air, causing my spine to straighten instinctively.

"Okay. What is it?" I asked, trying to hide the unease creeping into my voice.

"Between men." The captain's gaze flicked to Verena before settling back on me, and her hand tightened in mine.

"Anything you need to say can be said in front of her." I looked around us, but no one was glancing our way. They all seemed at ease with the tasks they were doing, a routine that they knew well.

"I'd prefer not to discuss finances in front of a woman." He said the words calmly, but I hated the way his gaze narrowed on her.

"Of course," Verena bit out in a tight voice, her hand falling from mine as she took a step back.

I desperately reached out for her hand, my fingers straining to catch hers before she slipped away. But instead, she simply nodded toward the captain, silently urging me to go.

"It's fine." She crossed her arms and turned her gaze toward the endless expanse of the sea. Its cerulean waters churned and crashed against the sides of the ship as if in defiance of the cloudless sky above.

My feet faltered as I made my way toward where he now stood, a few feet away from Verena's earshot, and unease settled heavily on my chest.

I was prepared to promise him whatever it was he needed to secure our passage on this ship.

I had feared that he would become greedier before dawn arrived, and it appeared that I was right.

I clenched my hands tightly in my pockets as I approached him, the sound of the waves crashing against the hull filling the silence between us.

"What is it?" I snapped, my voice laced with impatience and a hint of annoyance.

"You never told me who she was," he replied coolly, his eyes still fixed on the horizon. "I would have charged much more if I had known."

That sinking feeling in my gut turned to lead, and I could hardly breathe as I turned back to Verena, desperate to stop whatever was happening.

But it was too late.

A surge of dread coursed through my body as I caught sight of the King's Guards, their armor gleaming in the sunlight, charging down the docks toward us, toward her.

The rhythmic thud of their heavy footfalls reverberated against the wooden planks of the dock, creating an ominous soundtrack to the chaos unfolding around us. All other sounds seemed to fade away as panic consumed me, and I frantically looked for a way to escape.

Verena's eyes widened in terror as she saw them approaching. My heart dropped as I watched them get closer, my mind racing for a way to protect her, but it was too late.

"You bastard," I spat at the captain, my anger and fear boiling over.

I charged toward her, desperate to do something, but the captain latched onto the back of my shirt and pulled me back, causing me to collide against his chest with a jolt.

"Dacre!" Verena cried out just as the first guard reached her. He wrapped his hand tightly around her bicep as he jerked her backward and her eyes searched for me.

When they met me, all I could see was fear, pure raw fear in her eyes, and there was nothing I could do.

"Let her go!" I demanded as I slammed an elbow into the captain's stomach, but he didn't drop his hold. Instead, I felt a dagger press to my neck, my mother's dagger.

One of the guards scoffed at me as he stepped in front of Verena, blocking her from my view.

His sword gleamed in the rising sunlight.

"Who are you to command a king's guard?" he sneered, taking another step toward me with a smug grin on his face. "Who are you to defy the king's orders and take the heir?"

"He wasn't…" Verena started to explain, but I cut her off.

"I'm the son of the rebellion leader," I declared through my teeth. They were clenched together so tightly that I feared they might shatter. "The king's order means nothing to me."

My heart pounded against my rib cage, a fierce drumbeat urging me to do something, to do anything.

I lifted my hand slightly, but the captain caught the movement, his dagger pressing harder into my throat.

"If a trace of magic leaves you, I'll slit your throat before you could do anything to save her."

The mere thought of her enduring her father's cruelty once again was unbearable. The memories of her scars, etched into her skin by his brutal hand, clouded my mind.

She had confided in me about the horrors he had inflicted upon her, and I knew that if she was brought back to him, his wrath would be even greater.

She had run from him, and he would make her pay.

He had spent her lifetime trying to pull her magic from her, and I feared what he'd do once he found it. And if he did, he would stop at nothing to drain every ounce of it from her.

"Let me go!" Verena's desperate plea echoed through the air, but it fell on deaf ears as the guard pressed a sword to her neck.

"The captain here said he had a boy with too many coins in his pocket and a dagger that looked like it belonged to someone well above his station," the guard standing before her spoke. "Then you were foolish enough to let him see her. You brought the fucking heir to the docks and thought we wouldn't find out."

My gaze shifted to Verena, and I could see the regret and guilt swimming in her eyes.

"I never knew the king's men were capable of being so perceptive," I said through gritted teeth, trying to play off my fear with sarcasm. "Aren't you all usually ripping families apart and taking what little our people have to survive?"

"You insolent little…" He lunged toward me, brandishing his sword just as the captain roughly forced me onto my knees on the wooden dock. I didn't have time to react before the cold blade pressed deeper into my throat, a trickle of blood spilling down my neck.

"No!" Verena cried out, her voice laced with fear and desperation as the guards tightened their grip on her. "Do not touch him."

Her words were like a command, but the guard before her sneered his response. "You don't give the orders here,

Princess," he spat. "We have our orders from the king to return you to the palace, and that's what we'll do."

"Do not touch him!" Verena's eyes burned with a fire like I had never seen before. Her gaze met mine, and I saw a myriad of emotions as I searched her face, committing every dip, plane, and freckle to memory while I still could.

I could feel her power surge within me as her fear grew. I could feel it trembling in my own body as if it belonged to me as much as it did her.

And I couldn't stop thinking about the night before, about the things she had said, the story she had told.

I hadn't been sure before, but it thrummed through me now, making sure that I wasn't foolish enough to mistake it again.

Verena was my mate.

And I couldn't protect her.

She leaned forward, her body tilting slightly as she reached out to touch the rough wooden dock. The ship at our side rocked vigorously against the waves, mirroring the tumultuous anger in her eyes. I felt that same fury rise within me, allowing the anger to fill my senses just as her eyelids fluttered shut.

The sound of crashing waves and creaking wood enveloped us in a tempestuous symphony, making it seem as if the sea itself shared her wrath.

Then I tasted it, the salt water on my tongue.

I opened my mouth to call her name, to tell her to stop, but when her eyes opened again, I knew that it would do no good.

"Don't, Verena," I whispered, my voice barely audible.

If her father didn't know of her power, she might have stood a chance. But the moment she revealed it...

The wooden planks of the dock quaked beneath our feet as a towering wave surged through the sea. The frantic shouts and screams of the crew echoed in my ears, urging everyone to flee the docks.

My eyes were fixed on the churning water, its deep blue surface frothing with fury and danger. The sheer power of the ocean threatened to overwhelm us, and I could feel my heart pounding in fear and awe.

Verena's gaze was also fixated on the raging waters, her expression a mix of determination.

This was her.

"Verena," I called out her name again, but it was too late.

The massive wave crashed down against the dock, engulfing us all in its destructive force. The splintering wood, the screams, the sea—it all blurred together in a chaotic maelstrom.

I felt the icy grip of the ocean claim me, pull me down into its depths. I fought against it, screaming Verena's name over and over, but it was futile.

My back hit the dock, the crushing weight of the water still pressing down on me, and I coughed as my surroundings came into focus.

Verena was no longer held captive by a guard; instead, she stood defiantly, her hands squeezed tightly into fists at her sides.

There was so much anger still burning in her eyes, but she looked pale. Her power had unleashed a torrent of magic that had all but destroyed the dock we were on, leaving behind only twisted wreckage and screams of the dying.

The remnants of her power lingered in my body, a heavy weight that drained me from within. I could practically feel the embers of her strength burning out, leaving behind only a shell of who she was. Her exhaustion radiated from every pore, like a fire that had consumed all its fuel and now flickered weakly before dying out completely.

That exhaustion settled deep within me, making it hard to stand.

"Verena!" I called out her name, but the cold steel of the knife pressed against my throat before I could move.

"What did you do?" The guard behind me gasped as he struggled to catch his breath behind me.

"Let him go!" she demanded, ignoring his question completely.

"I'll slice his fucking throat." The guard spat as some of the others climbed back to their feet.

"If you make another fucking move, I'll kill him."

Verena dropped her hands limply at her sides as she looked at me, and I could see it in her eyes. She was giving up.

She was willing to give it all up for me.

"Verena, run," I called out, but she was no longer looking at me.

"Let him go," Verena demanded, though her voice was filled with desperation. "Let him go, and I'll do whatever you want. I'll do whatever my father wants."

I looked at her. Her eyes were wide with panic, and I could see tears streaming down her cheeks.

"Verena, no."

The guard's boot connected with my spine, sending me crashing to the ground. The impact was so forceful that I felt blood fill my mouth, and my vision blurred as I struggled to get back up.

"Verena." It was a plea, but I didn't know if she could hear it.

"Get him on the ship," I heard one of them command before I felt their hands on me, lifting me from the ground as I tried to fight against them.

My voice trembled with rage as I snarled, "I'll fucking kill you."

But the guard only laughed in response before roughly throwing me onto the ship's deck.

My body hit the hard wooden planks with a thud, pain shooting through my limbs. Through blurry eyes, I watched as the guard effortlessly cut the ropes that bound me to the pier, causing the ship to sway and rock. I struggled to lift myself up, feeling disoriented as I looked for her.

"You've got your reward." The guard shouted as the captain stepped onto the ship. "Deal with this damn traitor and make sure that he doesn't follow us or the king will have your head."

"Yes, sir." The captain chuckled as if he had no fear of the king.

But I did, and when I finally spotted Verena, she wasn't struggling as the guards surrounded her and forcefully pulled her away. Her eyes met mine, and a tear rolled down her cheek.

"Wait!" I yelled, attempting to crawl to her. "Please."

The waves crashed against the side of the ship, their rage deafening as they mocked my helplessness. I struggled to lift myself to my feet, the cracks and groans of the ship echoing my own anguish.

My voice caught in my throat as the ship began to pull away from the dock, and Verena's pleading eyes were the last thing I saw before she disappeared from sight.

CHAPTER 22
VERENA

The excruciating pain in my muscles was almost unbearable as we finally arrived back at the palace. Days had passed since we left Dacre behind on that cursed ship, and my mind was consumed with worry over his safety.

Fear and guilt gnawed at me with every passing moment, creating a churning turmoil in the pit of my stomach.

Dacre would never forgive me for what I had done.

My wrists were tightly bound behind my back as rough hands pushed me up the grand marble stairs of the palace. The rope had chafed my skin raw and every step felt like a knife digging deeper into my wounds.

My heart raced, threatening to burst from my chest. I was back in the capital city, gazing up at the towering palace that had once been my home.

But now, a wave of fear consumed me like a ravenous

beast. It clawed at my throat, constricting my breath. The air was thick with foreboding, making it hard to take even a single step forward.

This was once my home, but it was no longer. The opulent castle that once filled me with pride now loomed menacingly over me, casting dark shadows that seemed to whisper of danger.

As I was dragged through the halls, the memories of all that had taken place within these walls flooded back, each one more painful and terrifying than the last. I had been a prisoner here once before, the heir locked away for no one to see, and it felt as though I was suffocating as I was dragged back to that place.

I was led through the ornate halls, passing by statues of former kings and portraits of my family. There was one of my parents and I from when I was younger.

I had been foolish then, and I couldn't stand to look up at it and the way it mocked me now.

My mind spun with a whirlwind of thoughts and emotions, all centered around Dacre. My heart raced with a million fears, each one threatening to overwhelm me.

But I forced myself to push them down, to bury them deep within as I focused on the one thing that mattered: he was alive.

Dacre was my mate. I knew it the moment he said the words to me in that room.

I had told him a story, spoken a vow that my mother once told me, and the moment I did, I could feel the very fiber of my being change as if fusing me to him.

He had given everything up for me, was willing to leave this world behind for me, and now he was gone.

He was gone, I was back at the palace, and I could no longer feel him.

He had slipped away like sand through my fingers, and a dull ache settled in my chest as if he had been severed from me.

Both him and my magic.

It abandoned me the moment he sailed away, after I took that decision from him.

Or perhaps it had been drained from me when I commanded the sea to do my bidding, using every last drop of power within me until there was nothing left but ashes and embers.

But the guards had seen it, they had felt the storm I brought down upon them, and it was as if the ocean itself had stolen the air from my lungs, leaving me gasping and desperate for breath as I faced the terrifying possibility that I would never see him again.

He was hurt when that ship pulled away from the dock, defenseless against those I'd harmed, and I wished I could go back.

I should have listened to Dacre when he told me to stay behind. If the captain had never met me, never seen me, he wouldn't have had the chance to turn me into my father's men.

I longed for the safety of that room. It had been only him and me, Dacre and Verena, and I yearned for a world where that could have been our truth.

Longed to leave everyone and everything but him behind.

I closed my eyes and dreamed of his face. I yearned for the way he looked when he had called me his.

I was Princess Verena, heir to the Marmoris Kingdom, but more than anything, *I was his*.

My arms were twisted painfully behind my back as I was dragged into the king's throne room. The scent of incense and perfumed oils made me queasy as memory after memory flooded my mind.

"Your Majesty," one of the guards spoke, his voice trembling with reverence. Every guard in the room fell to their knees before him, forcing me down with them until my knees hit the hard marble floor.

I winced in pain as my bindings dug further into my wrists, but I stayed silent, though my mind raced with fear.

"Bring her forward." My father's command was calm yet laced with a sharpness that made fear grip me tighter as I was ushered to my feet.

Bile rose up my throat as I met the cold, calculating gaze of my father.

He sat on his throne, a regal and imposing figure, with his jaw clenched and his hands tightly gripping the arms of the chair. He looked at me, his eyes unmoving and unforgiving, and my stomach twisted with dread.

"Verena," he said, his voice cold and distant. "You have caused quite a fuss."

"I'm sorry." The lie I had told hundreds of times before slipped from my lips automatically, a learned response to avoid his wrath.

He looked at me for a long moment before standing up. "I am disappointed in you, Verena," he said, his voice echoing in the vast room. "Your kingdom is disappointed in you."

He motioned for the guards to bring me to him, and I was pushed forward until I stood just a few inches away from the man I feared most.

"Where have you been, daughter?" His eyes searched mine for any sign of deceit, any hint of rebellion that I may have been harboring.

I shook my head, my heart beating wildly within my chest. "Trying to get home." My voice trembled as I spoke.

Please believe me.

His hand shot out, slapping me hard across the face, and I immediately tasted the copper tinge of blood as my lip split.

"You have embarrassed this family." He continued, his voice low and dangerous as he leaned in close to me. "You have betrayed me, your family, your kingdom. I will not tolerate this insubordination from you."

Tears burned my eyes. "I'm sorry, Father," I said, my voice shaking.

"What would your mother think?"

I hated that he used her against me, digging his claws into the place he knew would hurt me the most.

"Unbind her wrists then leave us." His words hung in the air like a dark cloud, his face twisted into a mask of anger.

The guards unbound my wrists, and I rubbed at the raw

skin and dried blood. I faced my father, my eyes filled with fear and desperation.

"Please, Father."

He paid me no attention. "Send in Baelyn."

I whimpered as I heard the name of his healer, the healer who had healed so many of my injuries in my life, injuries that were caused by the hands of my father.

The guards began leaving the room, and tears burned at the corners of my eyes.

"Verena, I don't know what has come over you, but you must understand that your actions have consequences." His voice was firm as if speaking to an errant child. "I will not tolerate any more disobedience from you."

"Father—" I started but was cut off when the back of his rough, calloused hand collided with my face.

The pain was sharp and immediate, and I could feel the warmth of my blood trickling down my chin. "Verena," he said coolly, "learn your place."

As I stood there, my vision blurred by tears and pain, I knew that everything that had happened was leading to this moment.

Baelyn was led in, his eyes filled with concern as he looked at the state I was in. He approached me slowly, his hands reaching out to touch my face, but my father stopped him.

"You are not here to heal her. Not yet."

One of the guards who I hadn't noticed, pulled a wooden chair behind me, and my father instructed me to sit.

I did as he demanded and tried to steel myself for what was coming.

"They say the power came from her, Your Majesty. Not the rebel."

Terror snaked through me, cutting off my air with his words.

"The princess doesn't possess magic." My father's voice was low and dangerous.

The guard nodded, and I could see the fear in his eyes as he spoke. "I know, Your Majesty, but the guards who brought her in." He looked behind him as if he were unsure of whether he should say the next words. "They claim that she bent the sea to her will as if she were a sorceress."

My father turned to me, his gaze roaming over me as if looking for the magic they spoke of.

"What do they speak of, Verena?"

"I don't know." My fingers trembled as I balled them into fists.

He wouldn't stop until he got what he wanted from me. I knew that all too well.

My father's rough hand closed around my wrist, his thumb pressing deeply into the open wound where the rope had cut into my skin.

The searing pain spread through my body like wildfire, causing me to cry out in agony. My entire body trembled and shook as hot tears streamed down my face, my breaths coming in ragged gasps.

"Verena." My father spoke, softer this time, but no less menacing. "There are reports that you were inside the hidden kingdom. My men tell me they found you with one of those pieces of rebellion trash."

Terrified and desperate, I squeezed my eyes shut and took a deep breath.

"Were you in the hidden kingdom?"

My mind raced as he pressed down harder on my wrist, causing me to wince in pain.

The mere thought of Dacre's father filled me with a burning rage, almost as intense as the hatred I harbored for my own.

But even with all the pain his father had caused, I refused to betray the rebellion. No matter what torture he inflicted upon me, I would not turn on Dacre.

I would not give him Wren.

My father's impatience boiled over as I remained silent, and in a sudden motion, he raised his hand to strike me once more. His large, rough palm lingered in the air as I tensed my muscles, anticipating the imminent pain.

A sharp blow connected with my jaw, the impact so forceful that my teeth slammed together, the pressure threatening to crack them.

"Sir, if she's been there, then that means she knows the location of the hidden city," Baelyn spoke, his voice calm as if he were completely unaffected by the violence before him. "She knows the hub for the rebellion."

My father's clean-shaven jaw tightened before he looked me over. "You're right."

He reached out, and I flinched away from his touch. But he didn't stop; instead, he pressed his palm against my temple before gently brushing hair out of my face and running his fingers through my hair. "How useful you've become, Verena."

Useful.

The word reverberated in my mind, its weight heavy and suffocating. I had been reduced to nothing more than a mere tool, a means to an end for him to use in his ruthless pursuit of destroying those who dared to stand against him.

And now he was once again manipulating me, using me as leverage to try and extract information about their whereabouts.

"I don't know where it's at." The lie was so clear from my lips, so easy.

A tremor ran through my body as his fingers curled tightly in the back of my hair. His touch was rough and unforgiving, pressing against my scalp with a force that left no room for escape. My head tilted back, forced to look up at his towering figure.

"Verena, my dear," he began, his voice laced with disgust. "You are the heir to this kingdom, and although you may have been powerless most of your life, you are not stupid."

The weight of his words bore down on me like a physical force, making my lip tremble in fear.

I knew he could see right through me, as he always had. His keen eyes were like daggers, piercing through any facade I tried to put up. And when he struck me this time, I barely flinched.

Blood dripped down my chin as he tightened his hold on my hair, forcing me to meet his gaze again.

He moved closer to me, his face mere inches from

mine. I could feel the heat of his breath against my skin as he spoke with a venomous tone. "Do not lie to me," he seethed. "I am your king."

My king, not my father.

He was a king who demanded loyalty, never a father who wanted love. He didn't need my love; he had never needed it.

"I do not enjoy hurting you, Verena." His voice was low and laced with a hint of regret I knew he didn't really feel. "Don't make me hurt you more."

His fingers trailed down my cheek, leaving a trail of warmth before catching the blood that fell from my lip.

This was the moment I usually broke, the moment I longed for him not to hate me. These were the moments that I longed for my mother, that I damned the gods for taking her from me.

They took her from me, and they left me with this monster.

"I don't know how to get there," I repeated the lie, feeling it turn to ash on my tongue.

"And this power my men tell me about." He leaned closer to me until his eyes were looking directly into mine.

"I am powerless."

His grip on my cheek tightened, the pressure threatening to snap my jaw. He turned his gaze away from me and addressed the healer beside us. "Baelyn," he said. "Get prepared. The heir will need healing by the time we're through here."

READY FOR MORE FROM THE VEILED KINGDOM SERIES?

**The Rivaled Crown
is coming soon!**

Preorder now!

ALSO BY HOLLY RENEE

The Veiled Kingdom Series

The Veiled Kingdom

The Hunted Heir

Stars and Shadows Series:

A Kingdom of Stars and Shadows

A Kingdom of Blood and Betrayal

A Kingdom of Venom and Vows

A Kingdom of Fire and Fate

The Good Girls Series:

Where Good Girls Go to Die

Where Bad Girls Go to Fall

Where Bad Boys are Ruined

The Boys of Clermont Bay Series:

The Touch of a Villain

The Fall of a God

The Taste of an Enemy

The Deceit of a Devil

The Seduction of Pretty Lies

The Temptation of Dirty Secrets

The Rock Bottom Series:

Trouble with the Guy Next Door

Trouble with the Hotshot Boss

Trouble with the Fake Boyfriend

The Wrong Prince Charming

THANK YOU

Thank you so much for reading The Hunted Heir! I hope you are as in love with Dacre and Verena as I am!

Ready to fall in love with another world that I have created? A Kingdom of Stars and Shadows is a sexy, enemies-to-lovers fantasy romance that will have you begging for more! Keep reading for a sneek peak at book 1, A Kingdom of Stars and Shadows.

I would love for you to join my reader group, Hollywood, so we can connect and talk about all of your thoughts on The Hunted Heir! This group is the first place to find out about cover reveals, book news, and new releases!

You can also sign up for my newsletter here:
    Newsletter

Again, thank you for going on this journey with me.

Xo,
    Holly Renee

        www.authorhollyrenee.com

BEFORE YOU GO

Please consider leaving an honest review.

CONTINUE READING FOR A
LOOK AT A KINGDOM OF
STARS AND SHADOWS

A KINGDOM
OF STARS AND
SHADOWS

CHAPTER 1

I tried to swallow as the smoke from the burning embers encircled me in a cruel, slow torture. The royal army had been camped outside the cleave between our world and theirs for a total of three days. Three excruciatingly long days.

The grim tick of the clock echoed throughout the room, and my heart raced it before the next beat could sound.

My fingers trembled as I pulled my boot on my foot and tied up the laces. The room was as black as the starless night inside our home, but I didn't mind it. I welcomed it, honestly, because it was the only time I could do anything without everyone watching my every move.

"Where are you going?"

I clamped my eyes closed before quickly tucking my father's dagger into the side of my boot before she could see.

"I just need some air." I stood and pulled the hood of my worn-out cloak over my head. "Go back to sleep."

My mother wrapped her thin arms around herself and avoided my gaze. "Sleep alludes me." She shook her head. "You shouldn't be going out there tonight."

"I can take care of myself."

"I know that." Her dark brown eyes finally met my own. "But it won't be long now until they come, and…"

"And I should be able to enjoy my last few hours of freedom however I choose."

Her jaw clenched at my words. "They aren't taking you as a prisoner, Adara. Being the chosen Starblessed is a blessing from the gods."

"Of course." I bowed in front of her dramatically. "Look at the life it has afforded you."

She sucked in a shocked breath, but this wasn't a new argument. My fate had never been mine, and my mother had accepted many luxuries in exchange for her daughter. Luxuries that my father fought against. That he lost his life over.

I walked to the door and hesitated when my mother's trembling voice called back out to me. "Do not run. They will find you, and we will both pay the price for your treason."

I let her words skate over me and reminded myself of exactly who she was. My heart ached as dread filled me. My fate lay in the hands of the soldiers who waited for me outside the cleave, but I would mourn for no one that I left behind.

The cool night air danced along my skin as if it had

been waiting for me to open the door and slide outside. I pulled my hood tighter around my face to hide my curse as I stepped onto the cobblestone street and headed directly toward the place I should have been avoiding.

The streets were bare and quiet. Even the small pub that was usually overflowing with ale and unfaithful husbands was locked down tightly and not a flicker of candlelight shone through the window.

A chill ran down my spine, but I wouldn't allow myself to be fearful like they were. The Achlys family was powerful, but they weren't gods. If they were, then they would have no need for me.

I had never seen a single one of them. Not the king, the queen, or the crowned prince to whom I was sworn to marry. All I knew was that they were high fae and that the blood that coursed through my veins was somehow the key to unlocking their dormant power.

Lethal power they longed to possess.

To my knowledge, none of the royals had ever crossed over the cleave. They had men for that, and those low-ranked guards were the only ones I had encountered. If they had magic, I had never seen it.

My mother said they didn't use it here because they didn't have to, but part of me wondered if they still had any powers at all. If they didn't have magic, then I had no real reason to fear them. I could run, and my mother would be the one left to face the consequences.

Without powers, I doubted any of them would be able to find me. Only the twin moons knew my secrets as they watched me shift through the shadows. Everyone thought they knew exactly who I was, and that meant they all believed that I was the key to some blessing they thought the royals would bestow on them once I was sacrificed.

My fingers trailed across the bricks as I passed the last building and stepped onto the damp grass. I knew the path that led into the woods better than I knew my own home, and I let my feet lead the way as I looked around me for signs of anyone watching.

The edge of our town was only a few minutes' walk to the perimeter of the cleave, and I often liked to come here just to watch and imagine what life was like on the other side. It didn't look any different from the Starless realm.

The trees grew tall and heavy on both sides, and the only indication that the cleave existed was the thin veil that could hardly be seen at night. It reminded me of the mist that coated our land in the early morning hours, but the cleave never left. I crouched low and ran my fingers through the magic and a thrill of excitement rushed through me. I stared up as I watched the magic recoil from my touch, but it went on for as far as I could see.

It was hard to explain, but the divide between our worlds had felt more familiar to me than my own home. It felt like an old friend that I didn't even know. A familiar stranger that always greeted me.

Tonight, though, it felt different. Darker somehow as if it was warning me away. I pulled my hand back and searched through the gleam.

There were at least fifty soldiers camped in the woods about twenty yards from the cleave, and I watched the one who was standing guard at this edge of the camp.

His gaze was searching the tree line, looking for a threat, but he hadn't noticed me. I could easily cross the cleave and slit his throat if I dared. It would be far too effortless if he were only a man, but I didn't know what powers lay beneath his clueless stare.

My fingers edged toward my dagger as I looked past him and scanned the camp. There were several tents, all bearing the royal seal proudly, and a few soldiers sat by a large fire, laughing as they spoke to one another. I clenched my jaw as I watched them so at ease.

Soldiers sent here to take a human girl against her will, but that fate didn't seem to weigh heavily on any of them.

They were nothing but fools of a crooked kingdom, and my heart pounded in my chest as I watched them.

None of them sensed a threat. Not a single one of them worried about what the Starless could do to them.

But I wasn't Starless.

The twin moons shined brightly above me as my fingers traced over the rough metal handle of my dagger I had memorized years ago, but they tensed as my spine bristled. I turned to look behind me just as a gloved hand clamped down around my mouth.

Panic ensnared me as I searched the dark eyes behind me. His hand flexed against my mouth harder as if he was worried I would scream, but I wouldn't. None of these people would help me, and I didn't want to draw any attention from the fae soldiers.

They were already after me, and I didn't want them to know that I was watching them so closely.

"What the fuck are you doing?" his deep, sensual voice

that I didn't recognize growled at me before he dropped his hand from my mouth and jerked my own away from my dagger and tugged it out of my boot.

"Give that back."

I reached out for my blade, but he quickly moved out of my reach. He opened his hand and my dagger was enveloped in black smoke that dripped from his fingers. It floated in the air as if nothing was holding it but his magic. My breath rushed out of me as my marks hummed against my skin. It was as if the stranger in front of me had roused them from a deep slumber that I hadn't realized they were in.

"That's not going to happen." He lowered his hood, and my face flushed with warmth as I looked up at him. His jaw was sharp and his cheekbones high. His hair was black as the night sky and cut short. And gods, he was beautiful. High fae, I was absolutely certain. His ears came to the slightest point that always gave the fae away, but it was his unnatural beauty that divulged what he was so easily. That and his domineering boldness. "What are you doing on the edge of the cleave with nothing but a dagger to protect you?"

"I can handle myself." I had become tired of repeating that sentiment, but I still said it regardless of the fact that I didn't owe this fae any explanation.

"Can you?" His hand shot out and wrenched me forward. I flinched and barely noticed his hand as he pulled my hood back with a harsh tug.

His head jerked back as his gaze flicked rapidly over my face, and I knew exactly what he was seeing.

"You're the Starblessed?" His hand tightened around my arm almost to the point of pain, and my pulse raced beneath his touch.

"Starcursed." I lifted my chin as I corrected him. "You are a fae soldier?"

He didn't look like the other soldiers I had seen walking around the camp. His clothes were all black and held no marking of the royal guard.

He hesitated for a second before a small smile appeared on his full lips. "You could say that."

I didn't trust him. Whoever this man was, I knew that he was someone I should stay far away from.

"Let me go." I jerked my arm out of his hold, and his smile widened until his teeth were bared.

"What is the Starblessed doing in the woods in the middle of the night by herself? Shouldn't you be getting rest to meet your new husband tomorrow?"

Tomorrow. I was going to meet the crowned prince of Citlali tomorrow.

"I have a name." I turned away from him and looked back toward the camp. The soldiers there seemed none the wiser that either one of us stood in the woods just outside their tents.

"Adara." My name sounded like a plea from his lips.

I spun back toward him and searched his face. "I seem to be at a disadvantage. You know me, but I have no damn clue who you are."

That only made him smile harder.

"I'm no one important."

His answer grated on my nerves. It was nothing more

than a distraction. "So, you won't tell me your name then?"

His eyes narrowed and he cocked his head to the side as he studied me with a slow gaze over every inch of me. I wouldn't know the difference between the truth and a lie regardless of what he told me, but no matter who he was, he was strong. He screamed power without uttering a word. He could be the crowned prince standing in front of me, and I wouldn't know him.

"My name is Evren."

"Evren," I said his name aloud and savored the way it felt across my lips. "Are you going to be the one who escorts me to my prison?"

He jerked back as if I had slapped him. "You consider your betrothal to the crowned prince a prison?"

"I've never met the man, and yet my hand has been forced in marriage simply because he craves the power he believes my blood possesses. If that is not walking into a prison, what would you call it?"

He stepped forward, coming close enough to me that I could smell the hint of leather and something I couldn't quite put my finger on. I tensed as his eyes darkened and he clenched his jaw.

"You should watch the way you speak about the royal family."

Threatening. Everything about him felt like a threat.

"Or what?" I challenged and stared straight up at him as my breath rushed in and out of me. "They'll imprison me? They'll kill me? My blood is no good to them if it runs cold."

"You've lived a charmed life off the royal coin, have you not?" His tone was sharp and his gaze steady.

The urge to smack him was overwhelming, but I refused to let this fae see how badly his words affected me. "You know nothing of the life I've lived."

He was fae, and he couldn't possibly imagine the horrors that happened in our world. The Starless lived in poverty and fear. My family had been blessed by the starlight markings on my face and back, but we had also been cursed.

The royal favor had provided us with water and food to ensure I didn't starve, a roof over our heads to keep me safe, but it also stole my father from me. It stole my fate.

My cheeks and nose were covered in what looked like freckles if it weren't for their unnatural light golden color that seemed to flow against my skin. But it was my back that always shocked people. Those same markings cascaded down my spine in row after row of starlight, and it shot out at the edges as if it couldn't be controlled. Some edges stayed tightly against my spine while others touched the curve of my ribs.

Markings that almost felt like nothing to me, but they meant the world to everyone else.

"Perhaps, I don't." He lifted his hand, and for a second, I thought he was going to touch the markings on my cheek, but his hand balled into a fist and dropped back to his side. "Perhaps you are nothing like I thought you would be."

"But you have thought of me?" I questioned, my curiosity eating at me.

"We have all thought of you, Adara." He took a step

back, putting some space between us before clutching my dagger back in his hand and holding it in my direction. "You will determine the future of our world."

My heart raced at his words, and my fingers trembled as I took my weapon back from this stranger who so easily stole it. "And what if you're wrong about that? What if I am nothing like what you all thought I would be?"

He took another step back into the shadows of the trees, but I could feel his gaze still roaming over every inch of me. "I'm counting on that."

CHAPTER 2

The sun blinked into my window, and I groaned. It was far too early to be awoken by the false promise of a bright new day. Especially when I had spent far too long into the night watching the army and imagining what today would bring.

I had watched Evren as he left my side and made his way back to the camp. He moved stealthily through the soldiers who waited there, and when I took my eyes off of him for only a moment, he disappeared. No matter how long I scoured those campgrounds, I was not able to find him again.

It didn't matter, though. Evren was nothing more than a soldier who was there to do his job, and it was a job I hated him for.

Because today I would be seized from my home and taken to Citlali.

I tugged on my quilt until it completely covered my head, and I pinched my eyes closed against the reality of the day. I just needed a few more minutes to dream. A few more moments to think about what life might have been like if I wasn't born with a few spots on my face and down my back.

Starblessed.

What a damn joke. The stars hadn't blessed me. They had cursed me and my future, and I wasn't prepared for what was to come.

Last night was my first experience with fae magic, but I knew they were capable of so much more. I had been told stories throughout my childhood, but every one felt like a dark fairy tale. I had been told of how they drank the blood of the Starblessed to fuel their powers. A custom they had adopted from the vampyres before they had been banished from their lands. None of it had ever felt real, but today I would find out the truth.

Evren hadn't looked like the monster I had imagined in my head. He looked nothing like I expected of the high fae at all.

"Adara, it's time to get up." My mother barged into my small room and jerked the blanket from my body. She was dressed in her finest pink dress that fell over her body as if it were made just for her. Her dark hair was pulled out of her face and showed off the gleam that lay in her eyes.

"Mother," I growled as I reached out for my quilt, but she was already ripping open my curtains.

"It's reported that the royal guards have already packed

up camp and are soon to breach the cleave. You need to get up and get dressed. Today is your destiny."

My destiny. My mother was foolish if she truly believed that today was anything other than my death sentence. She was willingly handing me over to the fae, and she smiled as she moved about my room with no hesitation.

For a moment, I wondered what she would have done if it had been the vampyres who had come to claim me. She had told me many legends of the Blood Court that was beyond the kingdom of Citlali. Would she have given me over so willingly then too?

I knew deep down that she would have still sacrificed me for the life she now lived. The people of this town worshipped my mother. She had birthed the Starblessed with the largest mark in over a century.

She thought that made her special, blessed somehow, and I guess the reality of it was that she was right. Birthing me had afforded my mother a life she would never have been able to have on her own, and all that it cost her was her daughter and a husband she had supposedly loved.

"I'm up." I swung my legs over the side of my small bed and rubbed at my eyes. I was still wearing the same outfit from last night, and I figured my mother would complain about the dirt that I had managed to track into my bed.

But she didn't say a word.

Instead, she stared at me as she swallowed hard. "You need a bath, then I will do your hair. You can't arrive at the palace like this."

"I don't want to arrive at the palace at all." I pleaded

with my eyes even as I felt my heartbeat pounding through me.

My mother shook her head, but I didn't feel like begging her to choose me. There was nothing I could say that would ever make her change her mind about the decision she was making. Even if I could, both of us knew that the royals would do the exact same thing to her that they did to my father when he had tried to deny them.

And my life wasn't worth losing hers.

I pushed past her and into the washroom. She already had a bath drawn for me, and I quickly stripped out of my clothes before sinking into the lukewarm water. Tension eased from my body, but it couldn't stop the way my heart raced in panic with every passing second.

I slipped under the water and drowned out the world for a few short moments. I tried to reach for that feeling I got when I stood at the edge of the cleave far above the town where no one could see me. There was a sense of freedom there that I never felt anywhere else, but that comfort eluded me today.

Instead, all I could imagine was Evren's face and the way his dark eyes had studied me.

You will determine the future of our world.

Damning words that I wasn't ready to face.

I pushed out of the water and gasped for breath. I didn't know what Evren thought of me, but whatever it was, he was wrong.

"Here." My mother handed me a bar of soap and gave no heed to giving me any privacy.

She didn't leave my side again. Not until after I was

bathed and my tangled wet hair combed. She sat on my bed as we argued about the dress she had set out for me and how I decided to wear my pair of dark trousers instead.

She was angry when I tucked my black button-down shirt that had belonged to my father into the trousers, but I didn't care. She had made every choice for me, but I was going to wear what I wanted.

She offered to braid my hair and add a few flowers that she had picked from the field, and even though I wanted to argue, the anguish in her eyes made me sit down in front of her and bite my tongue until she was finished.

"You look beautiful." She tucked in the last flower, and I looked away from her before I did something foolish like begging her once again not to do this.

It was only a second later when a loud chime of the town bell rang out throughout the town and dread filled me.

"They're here," my mother whispered the thing no one needed to say. We all knew what today was, and we all knew what they came for.

I stood and grabbed my father's dagger from my dresser before tucking it down into my boot. My mother watched my every move, but she didn't dare say a word against it.

She led me back through our house, and I tried to take in every little detail as I followed her. The walls were worn and stained with years of life, and there were fresh flowers set on the small table only big enough for the two of us. I wouldn't particularly miss anything about it because it had never really felt like home to me, but it was the only real home I had ever had.

The place we lived before this, the home we had with my father, it was such a distant memory that I couldn't recall a single detail of it. It was nothing more than a feeling now, but it was stronger than anything I felt here.

My mother opened the front door, and I swallowed a deep breath as I heard whispers and some cheers from our neighbors. They had all been awarded just as handsomely as my mother for living with and protecting the Star-blessed.

As if any one of them could ever protect me.

They were all filled with fear, and that fear had every last one of them bowing their heads as the royal guard rode along our dirt road that led to me.

I held up my head in defiance as I stared straight ahead. I would not bow to some fake royals who thought they were gods in our world because they possessed a bit of magic.

They would take from me as they saw fit, but they would do so against my will. I was Adara Cahira of Star-less, and even though I feared them more than most, I refused to bend the knee to them.

I would rather die.

The royal guards stopped directly in front of us, and my mother fell to her knees before them. I swallowed down my disgust as I stared ahead at the guard who rode in the lead.

He watched me carefully, and his gaze dropped to my knees before his jaw clenched. He didn't reprimand me as he dismounted from his horse and moved around to stand in front of me.

"Adara Cahira." His gruff voice sounded as if he had spent far too many years with a pipe in his mouth.

I nodded my head once but didn't speak. My heart felt like it was lodged in my throat. I searched through the guards for Evren, but he wasn't anywhere to be seen.

"I am here on behalf of the house of Achlys to claim you for your betrothal to the crowned prince of Citlali."

I scoffed and looked down the line of the other royal guards. "They were too busy to come themselves?"

Shocked gasps rang out around me, but the guard's stern face carved into the slightest smile. "That they were, Starblessed."

I rolled my eyes at the name. I hated that name as much as the fate it damned me with.

"We are expected to arrive in Citlali by nightfall." He motioned toward the carriage that rode between the swarm of guards, and the dark black wood made me shudder with dread.

"How long is the trip?" I tried not to allow him to sense my fear.

"Several hours." He nodded toward my mother who still hadn't climbed from her knees. "You should say your goodbyes."

I looked down at her, and only after the guard took a step back did she rise. Emotion choked me as I stared at her, and I wasn't prepared for how affected I was by this moment. I had been angry with her for as long as I could remember, but I still wasn't ready to leave her.

I didn't want to say goodbye.

"Be smart, Adara." She reached out for me and gripped my hands in her own trembling ones. "Do what is expected of you."

I loathed her words. Every single one of them felt like a dagger to the chest, but I shouldn't have been surprised. That was all my mother ever wanted from me.

I nodded my head toward her once before pulling her into my arms. I didn't whisper words of love or fears of missing her because I didn't know if either were true. But she was all I had.

She clung to me before pulling away and tucking a stray hair behind my ear so nothing was out of place. Her dark brown eyes that were a mirror of my right one searched my face, but there were no more words to waste between us.

Part of me wondered if she regretted the decisions she had made as she looked up at me and saw the reminder of my father staring back at her in my ice-blue eye.

She had always told me that I was equal parts him and her. Half my father and half the woman who was so easily watching me leave, but she was wrong. I was nothing like her.

I stepped away and turned back to the guard who tilted his head in the direction of the carriage. I took the few short steps and ignored his hand when he held it out in my direction.

I climbed into the carriage and took a deep breath as the door closed behind me and surrounded me with the fear of my future. The interior was far nicer than anything I had ever seen in my entire life. The seat a supple black leather with satin red pillows against the wooden backrest.

I pressed against them before looking back out the open window. One of the guards was loading my small trunk onto the carriage while my mother gazed in longingly with unshed tears in her eyes.

The sight ripped at my chest until I noticed her hands clinging to a piece of parchment that was sealed with the blood-red royal crest.

I knew what that piece of parchment held without her even opening it. That was what she had traded me for. That was whatever she had been promised all those years ago when she had so willingly accepted my betrothal to our enemy.

The guards didn't linger, and they had no reason to. They had gotten what they came for, but I still clung to the seat as the horses lurched forward and the carriage began to move.

With panicked eyes, I looked back to my mother, but I could barely see her through the crowd of people that had gathered on the street. Most of them were waving at me with smiles on tired faces while others were tossing white wildflowers in my direction.

It was a sign of respect, something we usually only did to honor those who had passed to the gods, and dread filled me as I watched them hit the ground.

I traced the outline of my dagger as we began to pass by them in a blur. It was only a couple minutes' ride until we hit the cleave, and I anxiously watched my world fly by as I tried to steady my racing heart.

With every turn of the wooden wheels of our carriage, my fear spiked higher and higher.

I had never seen a single human pass through the cleave besides my father, and I was far too young to truly remember it. It is legend that passing through the cleave alters the Starless, changed forever by the magic that slumbered there, but there were very few stories about the Starblessed. The only thing I knew for sure was that it was said once you passed through, you shall never return.

It didn't matter how they were changed after they passed through the magic, because they were never going to return. I was never going to come back here after today.

I held my breath as we neared the edge of my world, and I slowly blinked them open once I knew we should have passed through. The horses didn't slow. They continued in their punishing rhythm.

I searched out the window, but the world around me didn't look much different from the one I had just given up. But it felt different. It was hard to explain, but it made me feel similar to the way I had with Evren the night before.

The smattering of marks across my cheeks and spine felt like they were alive, and my skin buzzed. It was as if the magic in this land sparked something inside of my curse to life. But it was duller than when Evren touched me. The magic of this world felt like a watered-down version of him.

I ran my fingers over my cheek as I tried to trace that feeling with my fingertips. It was foreign, but it also felt like it belonged.

I spent a long time tracing over those marks I had been

born with before I switched over to staring out the window. The scenery that passed us was so like that back home, and I soon became bored of the lush fields and dense forests.

I hadn't even realized I had fallen asleep until I was awoken by the stopping of the carriage. My hand shot out to catch myself on the seat across from me, and my heart raced as I realized I had let down my guard so easily with these fae males.

It was already dark outside, and as I stepped outside of the carriage, I realized that the fae sky was as starless as my own.

Only the twin moons shined high in the sky and provided what little light that they allowed. We were still near the forest edge, and I saw no signs of Citlali City.

"Where are we?" I asked one of the passing guards as I wrapped my arms around myself. Nightfall brought a chill along with it. Another thing that hadn't changed between worlds.

"We're about an hour outside of the capital, ma'am." He tilted his head down as if he was showing me honor, as if I was one of the royals that he served. "We tried to make it the entire distance, but the horses require water."

I nodded in understanding before stepping away from him and looking down the line of guards. There were far too many guards for the task at hand, in my opinion, but I assumed giving up this many men was nothing to the royals.

I stepped into the line of the dark forest and a chill ran down my back. The moonlight seemed to disappear with that one simple step, and I searched the line of black trees as my mark felt like it was flaring against my skin.

"Whoa there." A strong arm wrapped around my middle and jerked me back against his hard body and a step outside of the forest.

Evren.

My curse knew it was him before I could manage to put even an inch between us.

"The Onyx Forest is no place for a Starblessed. Especially not alone."

I looked back at him over my shoulder, and my stomach fluttered under his hold. "I didn't see you."

"That's because you were staring out into the trees."

"No." I shook my head softly. "Before."

"Were you looking for me?" A half smile formed on his lips.

"No." I told a lie we could both easily see through.

His hand tightened around me, almost involuntarily, as he stared down at me, and for a moment, we said nothing.

Evren had given me no reason to, but something deep inside me told me that I should fear this male. Everything inside of me felt tense and my heart hammered against my chest. But I couldn't bring myself to look away from his dark eyes even as that feeling sank into my gut.

"Don't go near the forest again without someone accompanying you." His voice was a hard warning.

"Why?" My gaze finally flicked away from him to look back to the quiet woods. "What's in there? Why are the leaves black? Are the vampyres this close to Citlali?"

My spine straightened at the thought. As much as I

hated the fae, I was far more fearful of the vampyres. Every story I had ever been told of them had been of their cruelty. While the highest of fae fed from the Starblessed to garner their powers, the vampyres fed from anyone they chose.

For food, for power, for pleasure.

"You have no reason to fear the vampyres here." Evren spoke softly above me and brought my attention back to him. "There are far worse things that lurk in those trees."

A chill coursed through me at his words.

"I am surrounded by enemies then?" I took a step out of his hold and tried to clear my head.

"You are surrounded by threats." He nodded his head once as if in warning and took a small step closer to me. He searched my eyes for a long moment before he lowered his tone. "You shouldn't trust anyone here."

"Even you?"

"Especially me." His eyes darkened and my stomach became heavy with yearning that made me feel like a traitor. This man was no different from the rest of them, and I would do well to remember that.

"Captain!" one of the guards called out, and Evren's jaw tensed. "We're ready to push on."

He looked over his shoulder toward the guard, and I watched as the young guard flinched. I wasn't sure if it was from respect or true fear, but my hands trembled as I watched the guard lower his head.

I couldn't trust him. He had just warned me of that himself.

"The future queen needs a moment." His voice was pure power, and it sent shivers down my spine.

It took a moment for his words to really hit me. I had known almost my entire life that I was betrothed to the future king of Citlali, but I had never imagined myself as anything other than his property. To hear someone call me the future queen, it messed with my head.

"Of course, Captain." The guard quickly backed away from where we stood, and Evren brought his attention back to me.

His gaze was still dark and domineering, but I couldn't bring myself to look away.

"We'll arrive at the Achlys palace shortly. You should prepare yourself."

"And how am I supposed to do that?" I asked breath-lessly. "How am I supposed to prepare myself for what lies inside that castle?"

I didn't know why I was asking him these questions. Evren was one of them. He was a high fae and loyal to the house of Achlys. But part of me was still desperate for his answer.

"You are the future queen of Citlali. Those who reside behind those castle walls will fall to their knees when they see you, as will all of Citlali."

"You didn't." I lifted my chin as I stared up at him.

A small smile played on his lips as he searched my face, and I could see his gaze roaming over every inch of the starlight that marked my face. "Trust me, princess. It took everything inside of me not to fall to my knees before you."

He slipped his hands into his pockets, and even though

I knew I should have retreated, his words made me fall impossibly closer to him.

"Don't call me that."

He lifted his fingers until they were only an inch away from my jaw before he slowly pulled them away. "You should get back to your carriage. The night is still young, and as the chosen Starblessed, you have much to face."

CHAPTER 3

"Welcome to Citlali," one of the guards said next to my window just before riding ahead of the carriage.

I scrambled to the side of the carriage so I could see the city that I had heard about since I was a child. Cobblestones thrummed beneath the carriage wheels as we hit the city streets. It should have been shrouded in darkness, but it was alive with bright lanterns that hung from the stone townhouses and candlelight that adorned almost every doorstep.

The residents of the capital city stood at their doorsteps and along the street as they watched our procession pass them by. Some waved while others simply tried to peer inside the carriage to look at me.

Some tossed flowers in the path that we took, but instead of white flowers of honor like those of the Starless Realm, the Citlali people tossed red poppies as they cheered.

And that reaction shocked me.

Almost all of the faces staring back at me were fae, but I noticed one man who bore the markings of starlight on his left shoulder. The marking was much smaller than my own, but he was the only other Starblessed I had ever seen.

And he currently had his arms wrapped around the fae woman in front of him.

He looked nothing like me. His skin was much darker than mine and his mark was so light that it almost looked white. My markings reminded me of the soft glow of the sun as it fell below the hills near my village.

Both of his eyes a light blue that matched my father's.

We were so different yet the same.

But he looked like he was happy to be here. Like he was in love.

I didn't take my eyes off him as the carriage continued through the city, and his gaze stared back at me as well. He had a gentle smile on his face, but I didn't return it. I didn't even know this man, but for some reason, I had the overwhelming urge to call him a traitor.

He was nothing to me, a complete stranger, but I still felt betrayed by the way he fit in so well with our enemies. I couldn't stop the deep ache in my chest even as the carriage turned the corner and the man disappeared from my view.

I had always imagined how the Achlys palace would look in my head, but my imagination hadn't done it justice. Even at night, the large building was striking, yet daunting.

The dark towers loomed over the town below, but most of the castle was hidden behind an imposing stone wall that reached higher than anyone could climb.

The carriage slowed as we approached the black iron gate, and my heart raced as the loud grating of metal rang out around us. I watched as the gate slowly opened to allow us through, and the urge to run hit me full force.

I knew once I passed beyond that wall that there would be no turning back. This was my fate, the fate decided my men and fae, not the gods. Only I could change it.

I could run, but I knew that they would find me. I shivered at the thought of what fate would wait for me then.

The fae soldiers I had met so far hadn't been what I expected, but I knew better than to provoke the fae of my childhood fairy tales. Evil, lethal, venomous. I didn't know if I had the courage to face those nightmares.

But the carriage moved forward again before I could truly consider it.

I was on edge, and I couldn't believe that it had only been this morning when I was taken from my home.

It had already felt like a lifetime ago.

The gate closed behind us with a loud clang, and my fingers edged toward my dagger as I searched out the window. The palace grounds were grand and beautiful, even though I had expected it to look like something else entirely.

The dark stones rose high into the sky, but glass windows were intricately weaved into the structure in a way that made it feel almost dazzling in the lanterns that hung within. Flowers caressed every inch of dirt that remained inside the stone grounds. Splashes of white and red everywhere to be seen.

The carriage stopped before a set of grand stairs that led

up to the even more imposing set of doors. I quickly checked my boot for my dagger before pushing my hair out of my face. I wished I had thought to bring my cloak. I felt desperate for the solace and privacy a simple piece of fabric could bring me.

The guard opened the carriage door, the same guard who had first approached me in Starless, and he once again held his hand out to help me. This time I took it. My hand trembled in his as I climbed out of the carriage and pressed my back against the smooth dark wood.

"Welcome to the Achlys palace." He bowed his head, but I wasn't really looking at him. I was too busy searching down the line of guards in the red and white uniforms, and I was only looking for black.

But Evren was nowhere to be seen.

The door to the palace opened with a deep groan that spoke of its age, and three fae women stepped outside. The youngest one with blonde curls that were thrown into a mess on top of her head, hurried down the stairs and kneeled before me.

I jerked back at her action, but my body was still pressed against the carriage.

Her brown eyes peered up at me, and I could see the confusion on her face. "Welcome, Starblessed. I'm Eletta, your lady-in-waiting."

I had no idea what that meant, but I was more than ready for the girl to get up off her knees. "Please call me Adara." I reached my hand out for her, but her cheeks reddened, and she quickly stood on her own.

"You must be tired from your trip. I have prepared your

rooms where you can rest until the king and queen are ready for you." She motioned up the stairs, and I quickly looked back in search of Evren one last time.

He still wasn't there, and I scolded myself for caring. He was a fae, a captain of a royal guard, and he would be no help to me here.

"I just need to grab my trunk." I started toward the back of the carriage, but the guard stopped me.

"It will be taken to your rooms."

My rooms. As if this was to become my home. I knew the reality of it was the truth, but it felt like the closest thing to a lie.

This palace would never be my home. It didn't matter what waited for me inside.

"Okay." I nodded and started up the stairs after Eletta.

She watched me with every step I took, but she didn't speak. We walked through the large doors, and I was instantly hit with the heat of a large hearth that sat at the base of the room. The fire was roaring inside as if it was trying to heat the entire palace, and I shuddered as I watched the large flames lick up the sides of the stone.

"Your room is in the north wing." Eletta nodded in that direction, and I followed behind her.

Everything we passed was gilded in gold or marble or beautifully aged stone. I had never seen anything like it in my entire life.

"How old is the Achlys palace?" I asked, and my voice echoed throughout the empty hall.

"It is said that the palace was built by the first fae king,

Novak, more than three millennia ago." Eletta absently ran her finger along the wall as she passed.

There was no way that could be right.

We finally reached my room, and Eletta opened the door before standing aside to allow me through. I did so hesitantly.

There was another small hearth at the edge of the room, and a much smaller fire danced inside and warmed the space. A large bed sat across from it covered in rich fabrics that draped to the floor in the softest shade of rouge.

As much as I hated it, my muscles begged for me to lie against it and feel if it was as welcoming as it appeared. There was a small desk perched next to the single window in the room, and atop it was blank parchment and ink along with a gold mirror that spanned the width of the dark wood.

"The washroom is this way." She stood near the only other door in the room, and I quickly followed her inside.

I couldn't stop the sigh from passing my lips as I spotted the large copper tub that took up most of the space. Eletta smiled.

"I shall prepare a bath for you so we can get you ready to be presented to the royal family. They should call upon you within the next couple hours."

"Okay." I nodded my head even though I was wholly unprepared for what was to come.

Eletta lifted her fingers and turned them in the smallest pivot, and water began pouring out of the stone wall into the tub. I shot backward and clung to the door as I watched her magic. The tub steamed with the heat of the water, and

I couldn't speak a word as she lifted a small bottle and dropped oil against the surface.

The smell of jasmine hit me just as she turned to face me.

"Are you all right?" She looked around quickly, reassuring herself that no one else was there.

"You used magic." It was a question and an accusation.

"Of course, I did." Her brows lowered, and she stuttered over her words. "Everyone here uses magic."

I stared at her because I wasn't sure what to say. Of course, I knew that the high fae would possess powers, but Eletta wasn't high fae. She was my lady-in-waiting, and I couldn't wrap my head around what I had just seen.

If Eletta could do that, what was Evren capable of?

"All fae have magic?" I finally managed the words as my hands tightened on the door.

"Most do." She nodded. "It's very rare for a fae not to possess any magic even if it is the simplest enchantments."

I was dying to know more. "And the royals, they possess a lot more magic than others?"

Her eyes flicked to the doorway, then back to me. I could see her hesitancy staring back at me, but she still spoke even though her voice was barely a whisper. "The Achlys family has passed down a potent magical line for the hundreds of years that they have been in power, but some worry that power may be waning."

I stepped forward, closer to her. "What does that mean?"

"I don't like to speak of this." She looked back toward the doorway.

"Please," I begged, and her eyes flew up to meet mine.

"It is said that the magic that lies within you will determine the fate of the Achlys family and all of Citlali. You will either be the key to their rise or the catalyst to their fall."

My heart hammered in my chest at her words. "I don't have that kind of power." I shook my head. "I don't have any power."

"Every Starblessed is born with the ability to awaken the dormant and lethal magic that hides within a fae. From what we've been told for years, you are the key to guaranteeing our safety." Eletta fidgeted with her dress.

Safety. "Safety from what? What if you're all wrong?" I clenched my fists at my sides as the weight of her words hit me.

Her eyes flashed with fear. "We should really get you into the bath, Starblessed."

"What if you're wrong?" I asked my question more firmly. If I was the one who was supposed to be such a vital role in the future of this kingdom, then I deserved to know the truth. Everything I had ever been told about my betrothal had been minimal and useless.

Never had I been told anything like this.

"If Prince Gavril feeds from you and he doesn't gain the power that is prophesied, then I fear that the kingdom will be truly vulnerable to Queen Veda for the first time in millennia." Her voice shook and fueled my unease.

I had never heard that name in my entire life. I had never heard of any other queen besides the one I was to serve. "Who is Queen Veda?"

Eletta turned and ran her hand over the rim of the tub. "She is the ruling monarch of the Blood Court, the vampyres, and it is told that she is ruthless in her power and her hatred."

A chill ran down my spine. I had heard legend after legend of the vampyres, and none of them were good. But I had never heard of their queen. "And she wants what?"

"To rule all." Eletta grabbed a towel from a small gold hook on the wall that looked softer than any fabric I had ever felt and set it beside the tub. "Queen Veda has wanted to overthrow Citlali for as long as I can remember, but this is the first time her threats have any real chance of coming true."

She nodded toward the tub, and I slowly slipped off my boots and set them directly beside the tub where I could reach them. Eletta's eyes widened as she watched me slide my dagger inside my boot, but she didn't say a word. I started to undress as my mind raced. "And you all think that I am going to be the one to stop her?"

I stepped inside the tub, and even the heat from the water couldn't cure the chill across my skin. I didn't know what these fae had been told of me, but I wasn't what they thought. I didn't possess the power to stop a vampyre queen. I didn't possess the power to stop anything.

"We pray to the gods that you are." She dipped a cloth into the water before lathering it with soap while I hid my breasts with my arms. "If the foretelling is wrong, then I hope the gods are truly watching over us."

For the first time in a long time, I prayed that they were too.

Printed in Great Britain
by Amazon